PINEAPPLE

TURTLES

A Pineapple Port Mystery: Book Ten

Amy Vansant

Vansant Creations, LLC / Amy Vansant
Annapolis, MD
http://www.AmyVansant.com
http://www.PineapplePort.com

Copy editing by Effrosyni Moschoudi
Proofreading by Effrosyni Moschoudi, Meg Barnhart & Connie Leap

CHAPTER ONE

One Week Earlier

Kim walked through the Marine Rescue Center, pushing Josh Jr. as he gurgled sing-song noises in his stroller. She flipped through turtle-stamped t-shirts on a rack one at a time, as if she were studying the designs, but her eyes didn't *see* anything but smears of dull color. Her vision had blurred and darkened. It was as if someone had wrapped a burlap bag around her head, and, strangely, *she didn't care.* It was a relief. The new gray-brown of her world kept her from screaming. She didn't want to remove her veil of sadness. It was safer, deep inside. Even her limbs worked as if someone else ran the controls.

Earlier, she'd been driving home when her arms jerked the steering wheel left, pointing the vehicle toward the beach and away from home. When she passed the Marine Rescue Center, she'd thought, *I should take Junior to see the turtles.*

That was the funny part: she wanted to take Josh Jr. to *see* the turtles.

She was inside the Center now, surrounded by rescued sea turtles lazily stroking inside giant tanks, when she realized how stupid she was.

He can't see them.

That's when the energy oozed out of her as if she were an overfilled sponge, and she walked like a zombie, pushing

Junior's carriage through the gift shop.

I'd nearly done it.

That was the other funny part. She and Josh had almost made it. There'd been a time when their fighting occurred as regularly as the rising and setting of the sun—and every other solar position on the weekends when he was home from work. Then she got pregnant, and *everything changed*. Josh was over the moon. He stopped drinking hard liquor in favor of beer. He started painting the nursery walls and building a crib. He spent *days* sanding the crib until it was as buttery smooth as their future baby's bottom.

Don't have a baby to save a marriage, her mother had warned.

Ha, Mom. What do you know?

The baby *had* saved her marriage.

She'd known it would. Josh had been talking about having a son since the day she met him. The day they found out it was a boy—

Oh *boy*.

The love kept piling on. She'd been promoted from Nagging Shrew to Queen Mother in the span of a few months.

Little Josh Jr. was born healthy. Check that off the list. Ten toes. Ten fingers.

A week later, work promoted Josh to foreman.

Could things have been any better?

And then today.

Everything changed today.

Had they not been grateful enough? What did they do to deserve *today*?

Josh Jr. hiccupped, and Kim looked at him without seeing him.

It was only fair. He didn't see her either.

Today was the day she found out Josh Jr. was blind.

One checkup and everything changed. Somewhere in the pit of her being, she'd already known it. There'd been a rock in her stomach for days, a creeping dread whispering *something's wrong*. She trained herself to swallow her fears and hide them from Josh and herself—most of all, *Josh*. She'd almost canceled the baby's checkup, but she knew Josh would want to know how it went, and she didn't think she could live the way she'd been living much longer. She *had* to know the truth, for better or for worse.

Ha. For better or for worse. That was funny, too.

The marriage wouldn't survive the diagnosis. Of that, she was sure.

She wished she hadn't gone to the doctor.

Stupid. Stupid. Stupid.

The way Josh Jr.'s eyes stayed fixed. The way he wouldn't follow a toy when she moved it in front of his face—

I knew it.

As much as Josh loved having a son, he didn't spend much time with the baby. When he did want to interact, it was easy to show him the *best* things. If you *booped* the baby on the nose with his stuffed lion, he giggled like any other baby. There was no reason for Josh to think his son couldn't *see* the lion. Josh wasn't the type to look into things too closely.

I could have hidden it for months.

For years.

Josh's mom was a different story, though. It wouldn't have been long before she noticed. Kim had already pretended to have a stomach virus to put off her mother's visit. How many times could she have the flu? A week ago, Josh asked if she wanted to have his mom watch the baby while they sneaked to the bar with their friends, and she had to fake a headache.

How long could I pretend to be sick?

So she'd kept the baby's doctor appointment, hoping to be proved wrong and put all her fears behind her.

But that wasn't to be. All her fears were with her now, fully realized, on top of her, smothering her.

Kim slipped her hand into her pocket and felt the card with

her next baby doctor appointment scribbled on it. At the next visit, the doctors would run tests to discover the cause of Junior's blindness, but the chances it was anything reversible were next to zero.

She had the time from today until that appointment, during which some hope remained that Josh Jr. could be a normal baby to enjoy her husband.

Then it would all be over.

Josh would be brokenhearted. The fights would start again. The marriage would end, and she'd be alone, raising a blind boy.

She still loved the baby, of course, but Josh—all he ever did was talk about someday playing catch with his son. The boy's room had so much baseball-themed décor it looked like Cooperstown.

And what if there were more issues? Who knew what else might be wrong with Junior? How much could she take? There might be something wrong with his brain. They didn't have the money to pay for expensive treatments. They barely had health insurance as it was. If Josh freaked out, lost his job—

She couldn't breathe. Something cried out. Color burst back into the world around her, but it wouldn't be *still*. It was spinning. *She* was spinning—

The cry again.

She clutched a clothing rack and steadied herself, listening.

A baby.

She looked into her stroller.

Not Junior. He rarely cried. He was a dream baby.

Emphasis on the *was*.

Kim blinked at the store around her. Some obscure power had pulled the cowl of dread from her eyes like a magician yanking away a silk scarf to reveal his greatest trick.

Ta da!

Everything became clear.

Kim's gaze settled on the baby in front of her. Another baby, one who could be Josh's twin, wrapped in blue blankets, sitting in a car seat, slung over his mother's arm.

A boy.

The baby's mother put the car seat on the ground and stepped in front of it to stand on her toes, helping her older daughter pull down a shirt with the Marine Rescue Center's logo printed on the back.

Do it. Now. Fast.

Kim grabbed the baby car seat and *moved*.

She balanced the seat on top of her stroller and walked briskly out of the building to her car. She put the car seat and the stroller in the back of the mini-van Josh had insisted they buy. She didn't secure them.

No time. They'll be fine.

Move.

Kim ran around to the front of the car and climbed into the driver's seat. She pulled from the driveway onto US-1 and headed toward the bridge that would take her home. The lights turned sea-turtle green for her as she rolled through each.

This was supposed to happen.

She glanced at the clock. If she went a little faster, she'd be sure to cross the Intracoastal Waterway before the bridge opened for boats on the hour.

Perfect.

A little trill of happiness made her shimmy in her seat and stomp on the gas.

CHAPTER TWO

Charlotte Morgan opened her eyes.

What was that?

She scanned her dark bedroom, the edges of furniture visible by the moonlight filtering through her plantation shutters.

Beside her, her soft-coated Wheaten, Abby, breathed in the rapid, *I'm-running-a-marathon-and-yet-sleeping* way she often did, two of her paws pressed against Charlotte's body to be sure she couldn't sneak away. She didn't know where Abby thought she'd go in the middle of the night, *but it wouldn't happen on her watch.*

Besides her dog's breathing, Charlotte couldn't hear anything except the steady patter of light rain outside.

Hm.

Something had woken her, but she couldn't put her finger on *what*. Maybe a dreaming Abby started tap dancing against her leg. Maybe she'd snorted herself awake. Both of those things happened with relative regularity.

She took a deep breath and released it, closing her eyes to start the falling-to-sleep process all over again.

Breathe in, breathe out. Breathe in—

Something wet struck her forehead.

Aaaarg!

With a yip, Charlotte scrambled out of bed. The sheets

tangled around her right foot, and she threw out her hands to brace them against the wall to keep from plowing her head through the plaster. Her other foot found the ground in time, and she jerked her right foot free from the sheets to have it join its mirror twin. She heard a thud, followed by the sound of scrabbling nails. Abby had fallen off the other side of the bed, half-asleep and as fully freaked out as her mother. She ran around the bed, ears perked, eyes wide, searching for clues as to why Mommy would destroy the *comfy sleeping* thing they had going.

Charlotte slapped one hand to her forehead. It felt wet.

Ew.

She turned on her bedside lamp.

Wet. Wet. Something wet on my forehead.

She looked at her fingers.

No color.

Not blood. Not smooshed bug. Not slug, salamander, snail, snake, or any of the other hundred things that might crawl across her Florida-based bed in the middle of the night.

She didn't know how other people in the country dealt with middle-of-the-night phenomena like these, but in Florida, when something unexpected touched you, you got *out of bed*. If what touched you was *wet*, all the worse.

But what could be wet?

She scanned her sheets and pillow.

Nothing moving. Nothing *crawling.*

With the tip of her finger, she flipped over the pillow and jumped back against the wall, just in case.

Nothing.

Abby released a little puffy *boof* noise to let Charlotte know she stood ready to help. At least, that was one interpretation. The other was that Abby wanted Mommy to know she needed to cut the nonsense and get back in bed.

It was hard to tell which.

Charlotte released a huff of her own.

"I don't know, Abb, I don't—"

She was about to drop to her knees and peek under the bed when something on her pillow *moved*.

She jerked back, staring at the spot through wide eyes.

The pillow *looked* clean and empty, devoid of creepy crawlies.

Did I imagine that?

She bent forward to better inspect the spot.

Nothing.

She touched the area.

It felt damp.

Water?

Her gaze rose to the ceiling above her bed.

A stain had formed on the formerly white ceiling. An amorphous brown swirl.

A leak.

Charlotte closed her eyes and tilted her face to the ceiling.

Ugh.

Great, it wasn't a snake, but how much would a leak cost to fix?

And worse, *should I do something about it now?*

Yes. That would be the responsible thing to do. Even though it was the middle of the night, it meant going through the dinky attic access and into the creepy attic. The last thing she wanted to do was climb into the attic crawlspace in the middle of the night. Attics were *unknowns*. There could be anything from a family of bats to the legendary *Florida Man* living up there, but she didn't know how long the rain would last or how wet her bedroom might become. Again, *Florida*. It could be a two-minute shower or the sort of thing that made Noah nervous. Checking the weather wouldn't help—they were only right half the time. Weathermen cheerily lied to her face every day.

If she waited until morning and the rain *did* stop, things might dry, and she wouldn't be able to find the cause. If she blew it off and moved to the other side of the bed and it *kept* raining, she might wake up in a swamp.

Crap.

Thanks, Nanny, for leaving me your house, but home ownership is for the birds.

Charlotte padded into the kitchen and found a small but powerful LED flashlight in the utility drawer. Abby danced alongside her, fully awake and excited to be on a rare nighttime adventure.

"You can't go into the attic."

Abby's trotting didn't slow, her toes tapping their message on the tile floor. *Sure I can. Why wouldn't I? Of course, I'll come with you. You don't even have to ask. I'm here.*

In the hall, Charlotte pulled down the collapsible attic stairs and headed up. Despite her previous enthusiasm, Abby watched her go, thwarted by the ladder's angle.

Charlotte poked her head up through the square hole in her ceiling, half-expecting a rabid raccoon to jump on her face.

Nothing happened.

So far, so good.

On her left, boxes sat piled across sheets of plywood. She'd dragged those wooden planks home from the hardware supply store, each cut to the exact width of the square hole attic access. She'd needed to create a stable floor if the attic would be useful to her.

On the plywood, she'd stacked boxes of holiday decorations, her suitcases, and a small collection of oddball things from her family she didn't want to display but couldn't bring herself to throw away. One really ugly lamp. An awful photo in a half-decent frame. A silver chafing dish.

What is chafing, anyway?

To her right, one strip of wood, barely wider than her foot, led off into the distance like the road less traveled. The attic's spine pointed to the small window at the far end. That was the direction she had to go.

Steadying herself against the low ceiling, careful to avoid the roofing nails poking through, she walked like a Flying Wallenda down the wooden tightrope, searching for the spot that intersected with the beams above her bedroom. From there, she inched along an even smaller piece of wood, the *two* of the two-by-four, toward the area above her pillow.

She squatted and felt around, finding the pink insulation wet.

Bingo.

Shining the light above her, she spotted a length of old plastic-wrapped wire with water dripping from its tip. She traced the path of the water as it led farther up the roof's pitch. It had rolled along a beam and then diverted down the wire, sending it directly to the spot above her head.

Naturally.

She tried to look at the sunny side of her situation. If the water found a path *behind* the drywall instead of dripping on her head, it could have gathered for years until the pocket became a riot of termites and black mold—

Hold on.

The beam of her flashlight struck a strangely square edge nestled in a nest of fluffy pink fiberglass insulation.

Hm.

Dropping to her hands and knees, she inched forward until she could reach the object, plucking at it until she'd jerked it close enough to grab. It revealed itself to be a simple white shoebox. She could tell by the weight something was inside, and by the sound it made when she shook it, it wasn't shoes.

Giving the area a once over with her light and confident the box was the only oddity, she crept back to the relative acreage of the spine.

Eager to see what was in her treasure box, she opened it there.

Papers.

Nothing that looked valuable.

Shoot.

So much for finding D.B. Cooper's money.

She returned the dusty lid to the box and carried it back to the exit. A red plastic Christmas-themed planter caught her eye. If there were ghosts in the attic, that pot was the reason. She'd killed *scores* of poinsettias in that pot.

Hm.

There's an idea.

Putting the shoebox aside, she carted the planter back to the source of the leak, setting it beneath the drip to catch the water.

Problem temporarily solved.

Retracing her steps to the exit, she lowered herself through the hole and shifted the door back in place.

Hopefully, the rain would stop soon. Tomorrow she'd have one of the Pineapple Port handymen come out and assess the situation.

Pain in the neck.

Abby jumped to her feet as Charlotte landed in the hall and stood sentry as she folded up the ladder and headed into the kitchen to get a better look in the shoebox.

Charlotte put away the flashlight and opened the box. It smelled like dust if *dust* was a smell. She didn't imagine anyone would be making *Attic Dust* a candle scent any time soon.

Probably somebody's old tax documents.

Flipping through the papers inside, the first to catch her eye was a newspaper clipping about a new resort opening in Jupiter Beach, Florida. The story featured a small group of employees standing in front of a charming, multilevel gray building with white columns and trim.

Maybe a box of vacation ideas?

The container contained drawings, math and spelling worksheets, and torn pages from yearbooks with row after row of smiling teenagers. At the bottom, she found a yellowing photo of a baby wrapped in pink swaddling clothes.

A folded sheet of paper pressing against the side of the box turned out to be the birth certificate of Siofra McQueen, whoever that was.

Probably the baby in the photo.

What kind of name is Siofra? Charlotte wasn't even sure how to pronounce it, but knew whatever she guessed would be wrong.

Charlotte did the math—if the certificate belonged to the child in the photo, baby Siofra would be forty-six now. She couldn't think of anyone her grandmother might know named McQueen.

The box probably belonged to someone from the family who owned the house before Nanny.

She was about to fold up the certificate when the birth mother's name caught her eye.

Estelle Byrne.

Hm.

The woman had the same first name as her grandmother, who raised her after her mother died. Soon after, her grandmother also died, and Charlotte was unofficially adopted by the Pineapple Port fifty-five-plus community and raised as their unofficial mascot. Overnight she'd gone from no family to hundreds of doting, if older, mothers and fathers.

The father's name didn't ring a bell: Shea McQueen.

Something nagged in Charlotte's brain, and she stared at the certificate to give the thought ample time to bubble to the forefront of her cerebral cortex.

Byrne. Byrne. Something about that last name…

Wasn't that her grandmother's maiden name?

She lowered the paper and looked at Abby.

"Do I have an aunt?" Once again, maybe she had more family than she ever imagined.

Abby glanced up and settled her head back between her paws, chin on the kitchen floor, her burst of midnight energy seemingly drained. She rolled on her side and stretched her legs straight as Charlotte flipped back to the top of the pile and reopened the newspaper article.

The grinning faces of the Loggerhead Inn.

A few of the girls in the photo were the right age then to be around forty-six now...

If her grandmother *had* had another baby, and this box was full of snippets from that baby's life, then her mystery aunt *had* to be one of the people in that staff photo, right?

Why else would the clipping be in the box?

Abby grunted to show her annoyance, and Charlotte looked down at her.

"I think you'll have to stay with Mariska for a bit."

Abby sighed, and Charlotte leaned down to ruffle the crop of hair sprouting from the top of her sleepy pet's head.

"Mommy's going to Jupiter Beach."

CHAPTER THREE

At exactly six o'clock in Targetsville, Florida, the Loyal Order of Gophers released a series of staccato belches to the recognizable tune of *Shave and a Haircut.* They flipped over their glasses with a deft hand maneuver rumored to only have been accomplished previously by the ancient Double-Jointed Pygmies of South Wallento and furiously thumbed their noses at the sky.

"To T.K.!"

The four men practiced for the Inter-Lodge Synchronized Drinking Olympics every third Wednesday night, and if another lodge ever started in the area, they were sure to bring home the gold.

Tommy Garth pulled his too-short *Dr. Who* t-shirt over his soft, hairy belly. Tommy's dark hair swept back from his forehead in a greasy pompadour. His ragged mustache resembled any one of several varieties of fungus and, in a pinch, could be used as a makeshift Rorschach test. Though he earned his living as a handyman, his true love was filming little stories he wrote while on the toilet. He kept a tablet and pen on the floor beside his commode and penned stories about men and women walking across their living rooms to poke a fire or answer the door and get the mail. The films contained no love, drama, mystery, or fantasy; people walked across rooms and cooked eggs or performed other mundane tasks. High art, he argued, *never* allowed anything of obvious consequence to happen. Not only were his movies devoid of intrigue, but he also buoyed the art factor by requiring his performers to complete *highbrow* tasks, like using a bowl and a whisk to beat scrambled eggs, instead of mixing them in the pan with a fork like a *commoner.*

Tommy couldn't find anyone to buy his films until he had an epiphany one morning during a particularly long commode constitutional.

That's when he started filming the actors in the *nude.*

Naked women accepted mail from naked postal carriers, naked men drank coffee and went to work for naked middle management, and naked grandfathers frolicked with naked dogs on naked hillsides.

Tommy sold an entire series of his naked films to a website entrepreneur who assured him they were 'great pop art.' The web guy even commissioned a dozen more custom films, though Tommy was at a loss as to why he wanted so many shots of *feet* in them.

"Finished up a great little film about dusting today," said Tommy to no one. "Lots of close-ups of bare feet walking back and forth. Some really good slow-motion work."

Mac Davies, Gopher treasurer, released a little burp. "You know that guy's using your movies on a porn site, right?"

Tommy gave him a side-eyed glance. "No, he's not."

"A porn site for foot fetishes."

Tommy snorted a laugh. "That's not a thing."

"Oh, my naïve friend." Mac patted him on the back. "You're an idiot."

Mac winced at his own words and regretted calling his friend an idiot. He was *trying* to become a better person. There had been a time when he was as happy as a physically fit, middle-aged, distinguishably graying man could be. His wife was the perfect homemaker. His dog never wet the rug. His goldfish didn't die half as often as some people's. His youngest son was a college baseball star and an all-around good kid who'd recently moved in with his girlfriend, Jenny.

It was when he'd discovered Jenny's given name was *Jake* that his world changed. When he realized "Jenny" had once been a tight end for the Crimson Tide (twice All-American), he marched to his car and tried to tear away his only bumper sticker, *"Have you hugged your child today?"*, only half-accomplishing the job. Now he drove around town sinisterly inquiring if the car behind him had hugged *anything* in the last twenty-four hours. He requested to be made Gopher treasurer instead of secretary, threw away all his pastel shirts, and subscribed to *Sports Illustrated, Soldier of Fortune,* and *Penthouse* before his wife talked him off the ledge.

He'd had a good cry, a long talk with his son and Jenny, and then vowed to be a better person. A *bigger* person. After all, he loved his son. What else could he do?

But being a better person was *hard.*

"You're not an idiot," he mumbled to Tommy.

Tommy grunted.

"No, you were right the first time," piped local Sheriff and Gopher Secretary (previously Treasurer) Frank Marshall.

Frank's only real cross to bear was a series of recent changes to his koi pond, which featured three statues. A heron, a fishing frog that *used* to have a cigar in its mouth, and for a brief time after angering a local teen by busting him for truancy, a Virgin Mary with a cigar in her mouth.

Bob Garitz, the last of the Gophers, wore too many sweater vests. He had a cold chest and really warm arms for reasons neither he nor his wife Mariska nor medical science could divine.

On the sleeveless sweater he wore for Gopher nights, Bob had pinned a medal he'd stolen from Major Hepper, commander of the old Air Force base upon which Targetsville now stood. Like the other Gophers, he'd spent much of his childhood watching thousands of yellow-grey dummy bombs fall to Earth with no more force than a bag of potatoes.

For the children of Targetsville, each bomb had developed a distinct personality. The missiles little Tommy watched fall screeched, "sweeeee KKKKKKkkkk," and Bob's bombs exploded "POW!" (Bob's bombs were stealth bombs until they hit the earth.) Walter 'T.K.' Weeble's bombs fell *Eeeeeeeeee SPLAT!*, something like how a falling tomato might end its life if it found its plump red bride picked by Momma Ragu and had access to a plane from which to commit suicide. Walter's father had owned the area's largest tomato farm, making him heir to a tomato dynasty and earning him the nickname The Tomato King, or 'T.K.' for short.

But now, the fifth and missing Gopher, T.K. Weeble, had passed away.

When the five Gophers had been children, they knew exactly when those amazing silver planes would drop their payload and when it was safe to collect the 'bombs.' Collecting dummy bombs was more interesting than collecting baseball cards, but they didn't fit in shoe boxes, took up a lot of space, and in the end, were pointless to trade and impossible to get autographed.

The teenage Gophers also killed time by dragging an orange egg crate to Major Hepper's window and watching him reenact "The Wounded Soldier and The Kind Battle Nurse" with his well-endowed secretary. They witnessed the Battle Nurse nursing him to health daily until one hot summer day, *Mrs.* Hepper walked in on The Kind Battle Nurse valiantly sucking the poison from the Major's freak snake bite, and the life of the professional bomb snatchers became infinitely less interesting.

Eventually, Hepper and his men packed up the Air Force base, the five boys grew into men, and the Gophers were born. Led by T.K., they spent their time bowling, talking, and taking the odd night course in woodcarving or welding.

They mostly drank at The Bromeliad, the Targetsville bar serving as their lodge.

Tonight, they drank to T.K., who'd gone to that great

tomato patch in the sky.

On this particular evening, none of the remaining Gophers knew they had one great adventure left.

CHAPTER FOUR

Charlotte glanced at her watch again.

Four o'clock in the morning.

Hm.

Well, all's fair if the light is on.

Leaping out of bed and throwing on flip-flops, she slapped across the wet road, the attic shoebox tucked under one arm, a light rain sprinkling her head.

She stood on her toes and peeped into Mariska's living room through the window. Inside, Mariska sat in her comfy chair, nose in a book. Her unofficially adoptive mother, the Pineapple Port neighbor most hands-on with her upbringing, never slept well. Most of the time, Charlotte felt bad for her, but Mariska's sleeping woes were really handy this time. She'd been in her own drippy home, staring at her watch, unable to get back to sleep in her damp bed, when she spotted the light flick on at her neighbor's house.

Finally.

Now she had someone to whine to about her leaky roof *and* explore the box of secrets she'd found in the attic.

Mariska had served as the closest thing to a mother Charlotte had after her mother and grandmother died. She couldn't grill her own family about the shoebox—not without driving straight to the Loggerhead Inn and starting the search for this possible, mysterious aunt—so, once again, Mariska would serve as her family's proxy. She *had* been waiting for the sun to come up so she could call the Loggerhead Inn, but for now, dumping everything on insomniac Mariska's brain would be a welcome interim solution to her inability to sleep.

Charlotte tapped on the window with her nail. Mariska didn't move. She tapped again, a little louder.

Mariska looked up and jumped in her seat, her hand fluttering to her chest, her book tumbling to the floor. She rolled her eyes and rocked herself to her feet before waddling towards the front door.

Charlotte moved to meet her there, and Mariska greeted her wearing a thin muumuu, squinting at her through tired eyes.

"What are you doing out in the rain? You just about scared me to death," she scolded.

"Sorry. I saw your light on and figured you couldn't sleep."

"I can't. My legs ache. Come in."

Charlotte entered, and they moved into the living room.

She looked around for the dog. "Izzy doesn't even come out to say *hi* now?"

Mariska shook her head. "She doesn't get out of bed this early for anyone. She's like her daddy that way."

Charlotte put her shoebox on the kitchen island, and Mariska peered at it.

"What's that?"

"You don't recognize it?"

"No. Should I?"

"No, I guess not." Charlotte opened the lid and retrieved the birth certificate to hand to Mariska. "What do you know about this?"

Mariska puttered back to her seat to gather her reading glasses from the table and returned to the island. She scanned the document and looked up at Charlotte, her expression blank.

"I don't understand."

Charlotte sighed. She knew by Mariska's expression she

didn't recognize anything about the document. If anything looked familiar and she didn't want to say, she'd be slipping on the strange, frozen mask she always adopted when lying or hiding something. It was as if she was afraid the tiniest arc of an eyebrow or quiver of a lip would give away everything. But, for some reason, she could never keep her nostrils from flaring. They were the true tell-tale.

Charlotte stabbed her finger at the line featuring the birth mother's name. "That's my grandmother's name as the mom, but that's *not* my mother's name for the baby."

Mariska's forehead folded into nubby rows. "You're saying your mother changed her name?"

"No. Look at the date of birth. That's not my mother's birthday *or* the right year." She poked at the father's name. "That's not my grandfather's name, and the baby was born the year after he died."

"I don't understand. Are you saying—"

Charlotte decided things would go faster if she left no room for interpretation. "I think my grandmother had another baby."

Mariska gasped. "*No.* Estelle always talked about her *only* daughter. This *has* to be your mom."

"It can't be. This baby is ten years younger. Mom couldn't look *ten* years older than she was. And who pretends to be *older*?"

Mariska sat down on a stool. "Where did you find this?"

"There was a leak—"

"Where? At your house?"

Charlotte nodded. "When I went to the attic to find the source—"

"It's leaking from your roof?"

Charlotte took a calming breath. "Yes. Where else would it leak from?"

Mariska shrugged in a world-weary way, implying she'd been fighting different sorts of leaks her whole life. "It could have been a window seal. Or under the door. Remember when I had that *river* coming through my sliders during that one hurricane—"

"Okay. Fair enough. But *no*, I have a roof leak. And when I went up to find—"

"I'll give you Jerry's phone number."

Charlotte stopped, her mind derailed from its gear by Mariska's comment. "Jerry who?"

"He's the roof guy. Those other guys will rip you off. You *have* to use Jerry."

"Okay. Thanks. But I'm trying to tell you—"

Mariska barreled on. "Greta used that outfit with the commercials. You know, the ones you see on the local news? They came out here and charged her an arm and a leg—"

Charlotte scowled and put her hand on Mariska's. "I'm trying to tell you about the shoebox."

"Sorry. Go ahead."

"Thank—"

Mariska pointed an index finger at her. "But use Jerry."

"I *will*." Charlotte decided to skip to the end of her story, hoping she could finish it. "Long story short, I found the box in the attic insulation."

Mariska seemed to ponder this new information. "Like it was hidden on purpose?"

"Now that you mention it, yes. Very much like that."

"What else is in it? Nothing that explains everything?"

"No. There are bits and bobs from schools all over the place...different states, different countries..." Charlotte smiled as she dug through the box, thinking she had to be the only person under thirty who said *bits and bobs*. Growing up in a retirement community, she used a fair amount of old-fashioned slang she rarely heard from the mouths of her 'contemporaries.'

She found the newspaper clipping and handed it to Mariska. "And there was this too."

Mariska looked it over before looking back up at her. "The Loggerhead Inn? What does this have to do with Estelle's secret baby?"

"I think the baby must be one of the people in the staff photo, but the paper doesn't name them. There are three women about the right age, though." She pointed to each.

Marisa pulled down her glasses and shook her head. "I don't know what to say. Your grandmother *never* said anything about a second daughter."

Charlotte sighed. "I had to ask. I thought maybe you'd know something."

"I'm sorry, I don't. This is all very exciting, though. Secret babies. It's like a Hallmark movie. Do you think she's secretly an angel?"

Charlotte jerked back her head. "What?"

"Someone always ends up being a secret angel." Mariska waved her hand as if dismissing her previous thought. "Probably not. What are you going to do?"

"As soon as the sun comes up, I'm going to call the Loggerhead Inn and see if Siofra McQueen still works there."

"You think she's still there?"

"I don't know. Right now, it's the only lead I have."

Mariska pressed her lips together and nodded. "It's all very mysterious. Any idea who Shea McQueen is?"

"I can tell you the Internet has no idea. I couldn't find anything about him—or at least nothing that told me I had the right Shea McQueen. I'm going to keep looking."

Charlotte spotted the exact moment Mariska's attention began to wander.

"Do you want some breakfast?"

Mariska's gaze drifted to her always-stuffed refrigerator. Charlotte was surprised the poor appliance didn't groan with relief at the idea of something being removed.

"I could make toast and eggs, or waffles, or a scramble, or—"

Charlotte smiled. "No, thank you. I'll do a little more research and then pack."

"Pack for what?"

"For a trip to Jupiter Beach. If I call and Siofra *is* there, I need to go meet her. If she isn't there, I want to look for her—find a lead. Can you watch Abby for a day or two?"

"Of course." Mariska frowned. "I don't know. Maybe Siofra doesn't want to be found."

Charlotte cocked her head. "I never considered that." She thought for a moment and then decided she didn't want to consider that scenario a possibility. "Ah well. I'll give you an update in a bit. Maybe I'll get her on the phone, and that's all it will take."

"Okay. Just let me know."

After enduring a trademark bear hug from Mariska, Charlotte packed up the box and returned to her house. She did more Internet searching but found no Shea McQueen who could be her grandmother's baby-daddy.

Nanny, what were you up to?

Why would her nanny have a baby with another man ten years after her mother was born? How could her mother not know she had a sister? Or half-sister, as the case may be—

Charlotte recalled a story her mother told her about travelling to live with a family friend on a farm for the summer when she was around ten. Enthralled by the idea of riding horses all day, young Charlotte had never thought it strange that her mother would be sent away to stay with a family friend she'd never met before or after. But now...

That's it.

Her grandmother had sent her mother to live with friends while she was heavily pregnant with Siofra. Her mother didn't know she had a sister because Nanny had hidden it.

Siofra had been a secret from the whole family.

But what about when her mother came home? Where was Siofra at the time?

Charlotte's gaze dropped to the birth certificate again.

Shea McQueen.

Did you take your daughter with you?

Charlotte looked at her watch again.

Eight o'clock.

Close enough.

She found her phone and dialed the Loggerhead Inn, which, according to the Internet, was still in business. The woman who answered the phone sounded young and chipper.

"Good morning, Loggerhead Inn. How can I help you?"

Charlotte decided to get right to the true purpose of her call.

"Hi, I was hoping someone there could help me. I'm looking for Siofra McQueen?" She pronounced the name 'she-fra,' which was how the Internet had told her to do it.

"I'd be happy to help you. Do you know what room she's staying in?"

"She isn't a guest. I think she works there."

"Oh." The girl's tone seemed to grow icy. "In what area?"

"That's it. I don't know. I was hoping *you* did," Charlotte said, tacking a nervous chuckle onto the end. It didn't seem to warm the chill growing between herself and the young woman on the opposite side of the line.

"Can I ask what this is about?"

"I—" Charlotte paused. She hadn't taken the time to devise a plausible answer to that question. She couldn't tell the woman she'd discovered she had an aunt she didn't know existed.

"She's a family friend, and I wanted to notify her about a death."

She winced. Her lie was a little heavier than she'd meant it to be.

After a short silence, the girl said, "Um, let me put you through to someone who might help. Just a second, please."

A few moments later, Charlotte heard another female voice, this one smoky, an older woman.

"Hello, can I help you?"

"Hi. I'm looking for Siofra McQueen."

She barely finished her sentence before the woman answered.

"I'm sorry, we don't have anyone here by that name."

"Oh." Charlotte felt defeated. "She was a friend of my mother's, and my mother's dead. I wanted to let her know."

"Who's your mother?"

"Hm?"

"Who's your mother?"

Charlotte frowned.

Do I have to tell her that?

"Um, I don't think—"

"Tell you what. I'll ask around and see if I can find anyone who might know her."

"I'd appreciate it. The name is Siofra McQueen. She'd be in her late forties."

"Got it."

Charlotte's attention wandered to the newspaper article, her gaze moving from one woman to the next. One possibility was blonde, the other two dark-haired...

Isn't it strange the woman on the phone never asked what Siofra looks like?

"Do you know what she looks like?" Charlotte asked.

"Who?" The woman sniffed. "Oh. No. How could I? I don't know her."

"I mean, I have a photo here I could send."

The line went quiet.

"Hello?"

The woman's voice returned. "I'm sorry. You have a photo of Siofra?"

Charlotte perked.

Hold on.

She called her Siofra.

Very familiar...almost as if she knows her...

"Yes."

"Recent?"

"No." Charlotte frowned.

That was another odd thing to ask.

"It's a photo of your staff on your grand opening day. If you give me an email, I can send it to you."

The woman clucked her tongue, sounding almost disappointed by Charlotte's information. "No need. I have that photo. It's been a while since I looked at it, but I'll take a peek."

"Great. I appreciate it. My name is Charlotte Morgan." She gave the woman her phone number. "And can I get your name?"

"Angelina. I'm the concierge-slash-manager."

"You've been there since the beginning?"

"Mm-hm."

"So I guess you're one of the people in this photo. Can I ask which one?"

Another pause. "Far left. Dark hair."

Charlotte dragged her finger along the picture until it rested on the chest of a glamorous, dark-haired, smiling, razor-thin woman.

One of the outside possibilities for Siofra. She'd suspected that person was too old to be Siofra, but it was hard to tell from a newspaper clipping. If she was Angelina, then only two other women could be Siofra.

"Siofra should be about forty-six, so if she's one of the people in this photo, that narrows it down."

"Mm-hm. I'll let you know if I can figure anything out."

"I appreciate it."

"No problem. Bye-bye."

The phone clicked dead.

Charlotte stared at the photo, her phone, and then back again.

Angelina knows more than she's letting on.

There were only a dozen people in the photo, all founding employees. If Angelina was one of them, she *had* to know who all the others were. Granted, the photo was close to twenty years old, but still...

I need to go to Jupiter Beach.

It was only a three-hour drive to the other side of Florida.

She called back the Loggerhead Inn and got the young woman again.

"Hi. I'd like to book a room."

CHAPTER FIVE

"Another round?"

The bartender, a tawny-haired young man named Ban with the wide-eyed expression of a man eternally goosed by invisible hands, stepped up to the Gophers' table. Ban was the first-born son of the only hippie in Targetsville, and his full name was Ban Nuclear Weapons Wright. His father, Fred Wright, a man known to the Gophers, had insisted on being addressed as Foliage Wright soon after his eighteenth birthday.

"Sure," said Tommy. He offered Bob a side-eyed glance as Ban walked away. "I think that boy's eyes bulged out the first time he heard his name."

Bob snorted a laugh. "I think it happened when he heard his wacko parents name his little brother."

Ban's little brother, Clubsoda Not Seals Wright, worked as a bar back at The Bromeliad.

Mac leaned forward to join the fun. "I think his parents took the drugs, but *he* has the flashbacks."

The group chuckled.

"Winner," said Tommy. The three of them toasted with a clink of their beer glasses.

"Remember the time T.K. grew that tomato in the shape of Jane Meadows?" asked Bob, staring at the empty chair at their table. Ban approached with a tray of fresh beers.

Frank took one. "Yep. What a talent that man had.

Remember him dressed up as Santa Claus on Christmas, puffin' on those damn Tomato-King-killin' cigarettes?"

Mac took the last draught of his beer and pushed away his empty glass to replace the coveted spot in front of him with his refill. "Remember the heroic way little Davy Thompson threw himself on T.K.'s face when his Santa beard caught on fire? Good thing he had the fire chief's son on his lap when it happened. I can still see him givin' those kids tomatoes out of his sack..."

Tommy rolled his eyes. "Givin' the *disappointed* kids tomatoes. Bless him for playin' Santa, but those kids didn't want tomatoes. They wanted Masters of the Cosmos men or whatever they were into then."

"Well, he meant well," mumbled Frank. "He got to the toys eventually."

They clinked their glasses.

Mac pounded the table with the flat of his palm and covered his face with his hands. "I love *women*. Did I ever tell you guys how much I love women?"

Tommy clapped him on the back. "We know Mac. You're doin' real good."

Mac sniffed and nodded. "I love my son, too."

"We know you do."

Tommy put his beer glass against his chin and sucked the air out to make it hang there. He held out his hands and waggled his head, the glass bobbing back and forth on his face.

Bob motioned to him. "That's a good one. We should add that to the routine."

An elderly man in a suit entered the bar and approached their table. He stood with his hands folded in front of him like a priest.

The four men looked up at him.

"Can we help you?" asked Frank.

"Good evening, gentlemen."

It sounded to Frank as if the stranger had a touch of a British accent, which didn't help to endear him to Frank. An exchange student from that country had once seduced his girlfriend in high school.

Tommy released the glass sucked to his face. "Man, you got great diction," he said, unaware the pressure created by his stunt had burst the blood vessels in his chin, giving him a ghastly red goatee.

"Thank you," said the man.

"You ever been filmed naked?"

The man's eyes widened. "Excuse me?"

Tommy sat up. "I'm looking for a guy to build a tool shed, naked. Or fry some bacon. Take your pick."

The man flashed an uncomfortable smile. "I'm afraid I don't understand, and your chin—"

"Play around with hammers and nails naked? I got one word for you: *splinters*. I'd go with the bacon," suggested Mac.

"But the bacon grease spits," muttered Bob.

Mac winced. "I didn't think of that."

The man lowered the finger he'd been pointing at Tommy and abandoned his attempt to draw attention to the broken blood vessels on his chin. "I'm looking for Mr. Weeble. I was told I could find him here."

Frank scowled. "No one but his mother and the I.R.S. called him *Mr. Weeble*."

"No?"

"No. He's The Tomato King. T.K. for short."

"Very well. Do you know where I can find T.K.?"

The men looked at each other, held their glasses aloft, and downed the beer-flavored air that remained in them with a single gulp.

"He's dead," said Tommy when they'd finished their toast.

The man scowled. "Is there anyone living in his house?"

"Elizabeth. She's still there."

"Beaver's still there," added Bob.

Mac punched him on the shoulder. "That's no way to talk about Elizabeth."

ɔb rolled his eyes. "Beaver's his *dog*, you idiot."

Mac sniffed. "Oh. Right."

The man shifted the weight from his left leg to his right. Elizabeth's his wife, I assume?"

Tommy nodded. "Yep. All the single women in Targetsville wore black to that wedding. Everyone wanted to be the Tomato Queen."

"Not Mariska," said Bob.

"She didn't grow up here."

Bob shrugged. "Still."

The man continued. "Any children?"

Mac nodded. "I got five. Want one?"

"I meant Mr. Tomato. Did *he* have children?"

"Oh. Nah." Mac didn't explain to the man T.K. and Elizabeth had tried everything to produce an heir, including one ugly incident with a box of Miracle Grow. He didn't mention Elizabeth had resorted to secretly naming the more attractive tomatoes after her immediate family. The man didn't need to know.

The man lowered himself into T.K.'s empty chair. The Gophers looked at each other and then glared at their uninvited guest.

"What can we help you with, buddy?" asked Mac.

"Can you tell me more about this Potato King?"

"*Tomato King.* T.K. was the *Tomato* King. If he was the Potato King, we'd call him P.K."

Tommy's head lolled on his neck. "What a man. There hasn't been a man like him since Jake Cardinal."

Frank squinted at Tommy. "Jake Cardinal? Why does that name sound familiar?"

"He's the guy who went to Canada to do Niagara Falls in a barrel filled with Fix-a-Flat."

"Oh, right. Right."

The stranger's eyes opened nearly as wide as Ban's. "Did he succeed?"

Tommy shook his head. "The barrel was undamaged, but Jake overdid it with the Fix-a-Flat and suffocated."

Mac nodded. "Tragic. Hey, why are you asking about T.K. anyway?"

The man pretended not to hear and motioned to Ban for a round of beers. "Can I get a round for the table?"

Mac opened his mouth to repeat his question, only to have Bob place a hand on his arm.

"Nope. Hold it. Free beer," he hissed.

The men remained strategically silent until Ban delivered the suds and turned to leave, nearly knocking over an old man entering the bar. The geezer screamed, "Herbert Vincent!" at the Gophers before pulling up a chair and sitting beside them.

Odd, unless you knew he'd been trying to remember his name all day.

Herbert stole Tommy's brand new beer, who in turn swiped Frank's.

"Here's a guy who could tell you the best story about T.K.," Bob said, clapping Herbert on the back.

Herbert nodded. "I grew up here in Targetsville. Back then, my front porch, living room, and bathroom were crushed by dummy bombs."

"Because your idiot dad built too close to the base," mumbled Bob.

Herbert ignored him. "One of the few *live* silver bombs ever dropped shattered twelve of my fourteen windows."

Frank looked at the stranger. "I think the pilots aimed for him."

"Probably," agreed Herbert, his chest swelling with what appeared to be pride.

Tommy picked up the story. "Major Hepper's replacement tried to evict old Herbert from his familial home with the help of a dozen soldiers. Standoff lasted two days."

Herbert raised both hands to pick up the story on his own. "On day two, I heard this low buzzing noise in the distance. Abe

Richard's blue crop duster appeared over the horizon and swooped low over the Air Force men. That's when T.K. released the bay doors and dropped a few hundred tomatoes on the heads of those bastards."

Herbert laughed so hard he triggered a coughing fit, and the others waited until he'd caught his breath.

"After all the press coverage, the Major let me keep my land," he added, wheezing.

Tommy took up the narrative reins for Herbert as he pretended to need Mac's beer to quell his cough.

"The story of the Great Tomato War grew larger and longer until legend had it that T.K., flying a shiny new B-52, dropped a hundred exploding red tomatoes, each with the wallop of a single hand grenade, on ten thousand armed soldiers and ten tanks, sending them off in such a fright the next day they offered to give all the land to T.K., who selflessly donated it to the town."

The stranger nodded slowly, his mouth pressed into a hard frown. "Well, I think I've heard enough." He squinted at the badge on Frank's chest. "Are you the sheriff?"

Frank nodded. "County. Why?"

"I have some papers for Elizabeth. Could you see that these get to her?" He pulled a manila envelope from his jacket and held it out. "I wouldn't ask, except I've tried to deliver them several times."

Frank took the package. "Are you asking me to serve her papers?" He slid the sheets from the manila envelope and glanced over them as the man moved away. "Hold it. These say you're going to rip up T.K's land."

The man shook his head. "*Our* land."

Herbert Vincent leapt to his feet, his eyes flashing white as his chair flipped over behind him. "You're not going to touch a *tomato* on that man's land, or my name isn't—" He fell quiet, the hand he'd thrust into the air slowly lowering as he silently lipped through the possibilities.

"Herbert Vincent," prompted Bob.

Herbert's hand shot back into the sky. "Herbert Vincent!"

Tommy stood, poking a finger in the stranger's direction. "I demand to know why you're here, who you are, why you don't like tomatoes, and if you have ever done any naked acting."

The suited man frowned. "I don't have time for this. I've sent these papers to Mr. Weeble several times over the last few months, and as the local constabulary, I was hoping you could help. We'll be at the vegetable field by seven tomorrow morning. I bid you good day."

He twirled on the heel of his shiny loafers and left the bar.

Bob looked at Tommy. "What kind of jackass says *I bid you good day?*"

Tommy shrugged. "I had a naked meter reader say it once in my movie, *Je T'aime Meter.*"

Mac flopped back into his chair. "T.K. never said anything about anyone ripping up his farm, did he?"

Frank reached for his beer without raising his gaze from the papers to find it gone. He took a moment to glower at Herbert. "Says here most of T.K.'s farm was on Air Force land, which was sold to this guy's company."

Frank looked up and furrowed his brow in Tommy's direction. "Your chin's red."

"Huh?" Tommy touched his face before weaving his way to the men's room.

Mac raised his empty glass in the air. "T.K., we won't let you down. We'll stop those bastards, or we'll die tryin'. Right, guys?"

"Look at my face!" wailed Tommy's reply from the bathroom.

Herbert stood. "Well, I'm going home. I have stuff to do."

Bob touched his arm. "You're going to leave T.K. hanging? After what he did for you?"

Herbert jerked away his arm and held up four bony fingers. "Three things. One, I'm too old for this crap. Two, *House*

Hunters is on tonight. Three—" Herbert studied his two remaining fingers and let one fall. "Three—I hate tomatoes. Make me break out. I swelled up like a balloon the night he dumped them tomatoes on me."

Bob scowled. "*House Hunters* is on tonight?"

"It's on every freakin' night." Mac huffed his disapproval. "Fine. You two go watch people whine about paint colors. Me, Frank, and Tommy will take care of Elizabeth."

"Yeah, you should go, Bob. Nighttime in the tomato field gets cold on the old arms," Frank added, plucking at Bob's sleeveless sweater.

Tommy pounded out of the bathroom. He had toilet paper wrapped around his chin like a bank robber who worked out of a men's room.

Frank stood, hiked up his pants, and left the bar together with Tommy and Mac.

Bob straightened his sleeveless sweater and turned to Herbert, who hovered near the table, unsure what to do next. "I need a ride home. Want to watch the show with me and Mariska?"

Herbert grunted and threw a dollar on the table. "She wear them stupid sweaters, too?"

CHAPTER SIX

"Hey, you."

Charlotte released Abby from her leash, and the dog froze, glancing back and forth between Charlotte's boyfriend, Declan, who'd just walked up the path to Mariska's stoop, and Mariska's dog Izzy, bouncing up and down to see her furry friend. It took Izzy leaping forward and slamming into her for the Wheaton to choose. Mariska opened her storm door, and without another glance at Declan, Abby and Izzy tore off into the house. Decision by tackle.

Charlotte smiled at Declan as the screen door clicked shut. "I was just dropping off Abby."

"Are you sure you don't want me to take her?" he asked, planting a quick kiss on her hairline.

"Nah. She likes playing with Izzy, and I won't be gone long."

Declan nodded to Mariska. "Good morning. Looks like you won the dog lottery."

"I did. Good morning. Would you like something to eat? Pancakes? Eggs? Maybe hash? I have some kielbasa..."

Declan held up a hand. "I'm good."

Mariska clucked her tongue. "You're so skinny. Both of you. I swear."

Behind Mariska, Abby flashed by on her way to sniff all the rooms in the house. Izzy hugged her backend like a squat, shedding tailgater.

Charlotte patted Declan on his perky pec. "Thanks for coming by before work. I wanted to say goodbye."

He nodded, looking confused. She imagined he was. She'd told him about finding the box and the trail leading to a mysterious aunt on the other side of the state, but the urge to drive to Jupiter Beach seemed sudden, even to her. She couldn't help it.

"So you think you might have an aunt in Florida?" he asked.

She shrugged. "It's a long shot, but I should try to find her at least."

"But the people at the hotel didn't know her?"

"No. At least no one at the Loggerhead Inn *admitted* to having any idea who she is, but it's my only lead. If I'm *there,* someone will have to talk to me. I can't shake the feeling they know more than they're letting on."

"I guess that's what makes you the detective."

She chuckled. "Or just a suspicious weirdo."

Declan slipped his hands into the pockets of his khaki shorts. "I looked up the hotel. Looks pretty nice."

"I wish you could go with me."

"Me too. But Blade's out of town, which leaves me with no one to watch the shop. Plus, I don't want to rush you out of there if you need more than a day."

She hooked her mouth to the side. "I might."

"I know how you roll."

They giggled together, and Declan looked at Mariska, his cheeks flushing red. Charlotte smiled.

Adorable.

"I'm going to head to work, but if you need any help with Abby, let me know," he said.

Mariska waved away his offer. "Oh she's a doll. Better behaved than Miss Izzy, I can tell you that."

"Sheds less, too," mumbled Charlotte. She threw her arms

around Mariska to squeeze her and then did the same to Declan. He shook a warning finger at her.

"Be careful driving. The middle of the state can get real remote, real fast. You might not have cell service, so stay on the main road."

She nodded as dutifully as she could muster. "Yes, sir."

With a final peck on the lips, Declan returned to his car and headed to work. Charlotte crossed the street to her home and grabbed her bags before hitting the road in her ancient Volvo 240 station wagon.

After filling her tank like a good girl to be sure she didn't run out of gas in the middle of swampland, she headed east on route seventy, snaking her way through cow pastures, tiny farming towns, and a plethora of pythons, alligators, and other miniature dinosaurs. The road dropped to a single lane for large stretches of the trip, and though she often found herself stuck behind locals doing barely the speed limit, she reached Indiantown Road, leading into Jupiter Beach, in close to three hours.

Once on the beach side of the bridge, she weaved her way westerly on the barrier island to the Loggerhead Inn, overlooking the Intracoastal Waterway. The place looked like a quaint southern home had stretched ten stories tall. The main building stood square and white, with charming porches dotting each level and flowering plants hanging like jewelry from the front of every room.

Charlotte pulled into one of the open parking spaces and jerked her duffle bag from the back. A flock of white ibis picked their way through the grass nearby, nabbing millipedes and throwing them back into their throats like kids popping M&Ms.

She watched them until she found the nerve to continue.

Here goes nothing.

Hefting her bag, she headed for the Inn. A doorman opened the door for her as she mounted the stairs leading to the long first-floor porch.

"Flapjack pants," he said, tipping his hat with a broad grin.

She glanced at him as she passed and flashed a smile she hoped didn't look as confused as she felt.

What did he say?

He remained smiling until she was inside and then eased the door shut behind her. Charlotte sensed *he* didn't think he'd said anything odd.

Okay. Shake it off. I heard him wrong.

She took a few steps into the foyer, her mind occupied, searching for a phrase that rhymed with flapjack pants and made sense. It took her a moment to notice a dark-haired woman staring at her from behind a desk fifteen feet inside the entrance. Above her, a fan with blades shaped like palms circled fast enough to keep the air moving.

As soon as Charlotte smiled at her, the woman stood and left the room.

Okaaay...

As she watched the stranger disappear down a hall, Charlotte guessed she'd been the concierge, probably the woman she'd talked to on the phone. She kicked herself for letting her get away.

Nothing left to do but check in.

Charlotte turned her attention to a short counter to the left, where a young woman somewhere near her age stood, smiling. A snake tattoo slithered up her arm, and her hair was as dark and curly as a Greek goddess's. Her name tag said *Croix*.

"Welcome to the Loggerhead Inn and Spa. How can I help you?" she asked as Charlotte walked closer.

Charlotte perked. "Oh, this is a spa too?" She hadn't noticed that feature on the website.

The girl shrugged. "It could be. Do you want a massage or a pedicure or something?"

Croix's expression seemed concerned as if she worried *she'd* have to find a way to perform these tasks.

"I—no. I just didn't..." Charlotte trailed off, feeling as if she'd gotten off-topic before she even started.

Why is nothing easy at this place?

She took a deep breath and decided to start over. "I'm Charlotte Morgan. I have a reservation for tonight?"

The girl typed something on the laptop perched on the counter and nodded. "Yep, I have you here for one night."

Charlotte nodded, but her mind wandered to the task ahead of her. She couldn't even enter the Inn without running into difficulties.

What are the chances I'll find my aunt before checkout tomorrow?

"Let me ask you, if I needed to stay another night or two, would that be a problem?"

Croix shook her head. "No. Not at the moment. But it's the beginning of the season, so be sure to let me know."

"I will, thank you." Charlotte glanced back at the little desk. "Is the concierge around?"

Croix's gaze swept the room. "She *was*... She'll be back." She busied herself sliding a card key into a paper case and handed it to Charlotte. "Take the elevator to the fourth floor—you're number four-eleven."

Charlotte smiled. *Four-one-one.* The number for information, and that's what she was here to gather. What were the chances?

She started toward the elevator and then, feeling as if she'd forgotten something, paused to look back at Croix. "Do you want to run my card?"

Croix snorted a laugh. "Nah. We know where to find you."

Charlotte snapped her mouth shut.

Why did that feel a little threatening?

She headed toward the elevator thinking the Loggerhead Inn was starting to feel a little like *Hotel California.*

CHAPTER SEVEN

"Just a second."

Shana Bennett perked in her seat and blinked at the officer speaking. Her eyes felt stiff and swollen from crying. She rubbed one with the back of her hand to untangle eyelashes bound to one another by salt and running mascara and then quickly lowered her arm back into place on her lap.

I shouldn't move.

She didn't know why not. She just knew she shouldn't.

The police had been in their home since an hour after baby Brody was taken. Her daughter had been whisked to her grandmother's house to shield her from the trauma of watching her parents fall to pieces. At seven, Maisy wasn't old enough to understand the gravity of the situation, but she'd seen her mother *lose her mind,* running around the Sea Turtle Center screaming and sobbing. She had *some* idea things were bad.

Shana knew she'd have to address the scene's effect on Maisy, but *later,* when Brody returned. Right now, for her daughter, it would be just another day at Mom-Mom's, making cookies and watching cartoons.

She and her husband sat on their sofa, huddled together, both of them praying someone would soon demand a ransom. *Anything* to know little Brody was still alive. Shana's body felt carved from marble. Something inside her demanded she hold perfectly still.

Don't move, and everything will be okay.

She feared shifting would break the spell, and Brody would be gone forever. When her husband pulled his hand from her sweaty palm to scratch his nose, she almost stopped breathing. She laid her palms flat on her thighs and held them there so he couldn't make her move again.

I might have already ruined everything, rubbing my eye.

Shana wasn't sure that holding still helped, but she did know one thing: *she'd never forgive herself.* How could she have left the baby on the ground? He'd been right behind her, less than a foot away—how did she not *sense* someone taking him?

The kidnapper was a woman. The police knew that much. The security cameras caught a glimpse of her and what looked like a stroller, but from what the cops said, they couldn't see much else. The woman parked so they didn't see her vehicle. She'd probably been planning the abduction for weeks. The stroller was probably empty, waiting to have a stolen baby placed inside. They didn't find Brody's car seat, which was strange. *She had to take Brody out of the car seat to put him in the stroller, right?* Maybe it fit inside. Maybe the kidnapper brought a stroller big enough for a car seat to fit inside *on purpose.*

Shana swallowed and wondered if flexing her throat muscles counted as moving.

Stop. The details don't matter. What matters is Brody is gone.

Saying those words in her head made the tears well up again, and she hung her head to concentrate and force them back. She could tell everyone was getting annoyed with her crying—her husband, the detectives—she could tell. Tears didn't help anything, but she couldn't stop.

She glanced at her husband, and he offered her a weak, hopeful smile.

He'll never forgive me.

This will be the end of us.

Carl had been calm so far—loving, supportive, offering words of hope when she needed them— but there was a distance to it all. He only held her hand to look supportive in front of the police, and could barely stand to *look* at her, the woman who'd lost his son.

If the baby wasn't recovered, he'd never forgive her for turning her back on Brody.

It had only been a few seconds.

The car seat was so heavy, and Maisy needed help—

She felt the sofa cushion bounce as Carl straightened.

"What is it?" he asked the officer.

She looked up.

He saw something. Something's happening.

Detective Jimenez held a cell phone to his ear. She hadn't heard it ring. Jimenez acknowledged Carl's question by holding up a finger, asking for a moment. A few seconds later, he said *Got it, okay, okay, bye* and lowered the phone to his side. He looked at them and smiled.

He's smiling. What does that mean?

Shana felt hope flutter in her chest.

"They're returning him," said Jimenez.

"What?" Shana almost whispered the word, more afraid to move now than ever. She couldn't help it.

"You have him?" asked Carl.

Shana nodded. That was the question to ask.

I should have asked that.

Jimenez shook his head, but he raised a palm as if to say, *I'm going to say 'no,' but don't be alarmed.*

"Not yet," is what he did say. "Someone called the station and said they were leaving the baby for us to pick up."

"Where? Why? Who steals a baby just to give it back?" asked Carl.

Shana's arm shot out before she could stop it, and she slapped her husband in the middle of his chest with the back of her hand.

"Who *cares*? Why would you ask that? You're going to jinx *everything!*"

He looked at her as if she wasn't someone he recognized, and she realized how crazy she must appear between the tears, the swollen eyes, and the *rage* that shot through her upon hearing Carl's stupid, *stupid* question.

"I just mean, it's strange, isn't it? To steal a baby and then give it back?" he mumbled.

Jimenez shook his head. "You'd be surprised. It isn't that weird for someone to change their mind about something bad they did."

Shana felt her fear turning to anger. *Horrible woman... Who is this horrible woman who would put us through this just to change her mind?*

She looked up. Everyone was staring at her.

I said it out loud.

She knew then she'd said her angry thoughts aloud, but she didn't say *woman*. She'd said a much worse word. The sort of word she'd trained herself not to say anymore now that she'd moved into Carl's world.

Carl frowned at her. He didn't like it when she reminded him of her modest beginnings. She was his wife now. She had to remember to act accordingly.

Her baby had been *taken*. What did he expect? Maybe he shouldn't have dated his waitress if he felt—

She made a fist and pushed her fingernails into her palm to stop her thoughts.

Stop. Stop. Think about Brody.

She forced her attention to Jimenez. "Can we go? Can we go get Brody?"

"We've got officers en route. It's safer this way."

"I can't stand it." Shana dropped her head into her hands. For some reason, the rule about moving had expired in her head. "I can't just sit here—"

Jimenez' phone rang, and he answered. Shana and Carl locked gazes on him as if they had targeting systems built into their brains.

"What is it? Do they have him?" Shana stood as he ended his call. She gripped Jimenez' free arm so he couldn't avoid answering. Carl tried to grab her other hand to pull her back down to her seat, and she jerked it out of his reach.

Jimenez put his phone on the table and put his hand on the fingers she used to clutch his sleeve.

"We have him."

Shana felt her legs go wobbly. She squatted to the ground to keep from falling. "Oh, thank God, thank you, Jesus. Thank you, *thank you*."

Carl shook the detective's hand and helped Shana back to the sofa. She knew it embarrassed him to see her squatting at the detective's feet, but all the strength had left her legs.

"Can we see him now?" she asked.

"Sure. Sure. They're taking him to the hospital—"

Shana felt another wave of dread rise in her chest. "He's hurt?"

"No, *no*—sorry. They just have to check him out. Standard procedure. I'll take you there."

He led them to his cruiser. As Shana and Carl walked, gripping each other's arms, Jimenez explained how they'd meet the other officers at the hospital. Their apparently unharmed baby would be examined as a safety precaution.

The drive took *forever,* but Shana felt as light as air as she entered the hospital. She knew in a few moments, she'd be holding little Brody in her arms again, kissing his fat little chipmunk cheeks. Her mistake was erased, and the weight of this most horrible day had lifted from her shoulders. Carl wouldn't hold it against her now. They would fall back into their roles, and everything would be fine. She'd never take her eyes off Brody again.

She turned into the examination room, trying hard not to break into a sprint.

There he was with the doctor, gurgling, happy.

Brody.

My beautiful boy.

She dove to take him, and Carl grabbed her arm. "Wait, honey, wait until—"

She flashed him a look that said *touch me again. I dare you.*

He lowered his hand and offered the doctor an apologetic look.

She knew then she had the power back.

Everything is back to normal.

"He's fine," said the doctor, handing Brody to Shana. "The baby's unharmed."

Shana scooped Brody into her arms and held him tight against her chest.

"Oh baby, oh baby, I'm so sorry."

She lowered him to stare into his gurgling face.

Brody. Brody. Brody—

The realization started as a creeping *prickle*, working its way up her neck like a praying mantis making its way up her spine.

Something's wrong.

Brody's smell was off. Maybe they'd used a different product on him?

No. It wasn't only his smell.

Something about his eyes is wrong.

From the very first day, when the nurses insisted he couldn't even focus, he stared right into her eyes. They weren't the right shade, but more than that, he refused to look at her. He always looked at her. Brody always stared right into her face and grabbed for her nose. It was one of their things.

She looked at the doctor.

"What's wrong with his eyes?" she asked, hoping he had an explanation.

But she could already feel the chant starting in her head.

No. No. No.

The doctor smiled. "Well, he's still blind, of course."

Blind? Shana shrieked the word in her head, but her lips

never opened. They couldn't—she felt frozen again.

Carl said the word out loud. "Blind?"

The doctor scowled. "You didn't know?"

Shana looked at the baby. She could see it now. She could see it everywhere. His hair wasn't as sandy, and his nose was broader. She turned him over and pulled down his cheap little pants, not the ones they'd bought for him during their last trip to Palm Beach. Not the ones he'd been wearing.

The freckle above his right butt cheek is missing.

The world began to swim around Shana.

"It isn't Brody."

Someone snatched the baby from her arms as she fell.

CHAPTER EIGHT

After individually checking in with their families, Frank, Mac, and Tommy drove to T.K.'s house and knocked on what was now only his wife Elizabeth's door. No one answered.

"She's asleep. Knock harder," suggested Mac.

Frank frowned and glanced at his watch. It was nearly ten. "Nah. I don't want to wake her just to upset her. We'll come back in the morning."

"What if that guy gets here first?" asked Tommy.

Frank paused. "He said seven in the morning, didn't he?"

"He might have lied."

Frank ran his hand over his thinning hair. "What does that mean? Are you suggesting we sleep in her back yard?"

Mac hooked a thumb toward the large gravel driveway. "We could sleep in our cars."

Frank chewed on his lip. He didn't relish the idea of sleeping in his cruiser. On the other hand, he didn't know what the stranger might be up to—big corporations could be slippery. They might sneak over in the middle of the night and establish some sort of claim to T.K.'s land, and with the King gone, he felt a need to protect Elizabeth from the jackals out to steal her land.

He huffed a sigh. "Fine. I'll stay here. You guys can go home."

Tommy and Mac both shook their heads.

"Nope. We'll stick it out with you," said Tommy.

Frank noted the light in T.K.'s back yard was dim enough he didn't have to stare at his friend's bruised chin anymore. "There's no point—"

Mac held up a hand to silence him. "Wouldn't have it any other way."

Frank shrugged. "Suit yourself."

They walked to their cars and crawled inside to sleep. From the back seat of his cruiser, Frank called his wife, Darla.

"Turns out I'm not coming home tonight," he said when she answered. She sounded sleepy.

"Tell her to come get your laundry," she mumbled.

Frank chuckled. "I'm not cheating on you. I told you there's trouble out at T.K.'s farm. I have to be here at the crack of dawn, so there's no point in coming home and trying to get any sleep. I'm a little worried they might try and sneak in early."

He heard Darla grunt, and he could picture her sitting up in bed.

"Remind me again? T.K.'s your Gopher friend who died?" she asked.

"I told you."

"I don't really listen to you."

Frank sighed. "Yeah. This big company's trying to take his land. Me, Mac, and Tommy are out here to stop them."

"Why?"

"To help his wife and family—"

"No, I mean, why is some company trying to take his land?"

"Oh. I dunno. We'll get it worked out tomorrow. I'll delay them until I can get hold of a judge. Get an injunction or something."

"Okay. Whatever. What about Bob? Is he still with you?"

"Last I heard, he and Herbert were going to Bob's to watch *House Hunters*."

Darla laughed. "Mariska will *kill* those drunken idiots if they show up this late."

"If you see Bob tomorrow, tell him to come out with as

many bodies as he can bring. We might have to block the tractors or something."

"Recruit people to throw themselves in front of tractors. Got it. I'll get right on that. Good night."

"Good night."

Frank hung up and tried to find a comfortable position in his car. He grunted and rolled from one side to the other.

The back seat of a police cruiser isn't built for comfort. Who'd have thought?

Frank awoke at two, his right knee aching. The back seat wasn't long enough, and he'd been sleeping in a fetal position.

This isn't going to work.

Unable to find a comfortable alternative, he left the car and wandered to a hammock hanging between two palm trees in the corner of T.K's back yard. He crawled inside of it, and it sagged to within an inch above the ground.

He held his breath, waiting for it to collapse.

It didn't.

Good enough.

He nodded off. He lounged on the tropical sands in his dreams with a beautiful long-haired girl. She lay beside him, and he could feel her dark, furry hair touching his cheek—

Wait a second.

Frank pressed his mental rewind button and replayed. Tropical beach. Beautiful girl. Dark, furry hair against his—

That was it.

Furry.

That's not right.

He opened his lids and saw a dark eye peering at him so close he could touch it.

He let out a *whoop!*

Mac and Tommy sat straight up on the ground beside him and took a token swing at each other, whiffing by a foot. Their movement scared Frank all over again, and he let out another yelp before his mind and T.K.'s back porch light clued him where he was, and the pieces began to fall together.

"What? What is it?" asked Tommy, panting.

Frank fought to sit up in the low-slung hammock. "What are you two doing out here?"

"We both got up to pee simultaneously, saw you over here, and decided we'd better set up camp next to you."

"On the *ground*?"

Tommy shrugged. "You already had the hammock."

"Why're you screaming?" asked Mac.

Frank closed his eyes and thought about the eye he'd seen. One eye, big, dark, on the side of a head...he ran through the possibilities until he'd narrowed them down to one suspect.

"*Rabbit*. I think. He was goin' for my earlobe. I woke up just in time."

Mac shook his head. "Jeeze, Frank, I nearly had a heart attack."

Frank peered at his watch. It was five-thirty. His hip ached, and the early morning dew had added fifteen pounds to his uniform. He shivered in the already eighty-degree heat. His body still pulsed from the adrenaline dumped by the rabbit's visit.

"Floppy-eared, bloodthirsty sonuva—if I'd had my gun—"

Mac chuckled. "Good thing you didn't. You probably would have killed us all."

Frank clambered out of the hammock and stretched before finding a discreet spot behind a tree to relieve his bladder. When he returned to the others, he motioned to Tommy. "You're up. Why don't you make yourself useful and get us some breakfast?"

"Good idea." Tommy headed off in the direction of T.K's house.

Mac handed Frank the folded piece of dark green plastic he'd been sleeping on. "Here. Take this to sit on. Ground's all wet."

"What is it? A trash bag?"

Mac shook his head. "*Used* to be a trash bag. My wife sews them into rain slickers. I had a bunch in my trunk. I was supposed to try and sell them to the guys at work."

"But you gave her the money and kept them to avoid the embarrassment of letting your co-workers know your wife makes slickers out of trashbags?"

Mac nodded. "Yup. I can see why you're the sheriff."

They sat on the ground facing each other, arms wrapped around their knees.

"My bones hurt, and my clothes are soaked," muttered Frank.

"Yep. This was a bad idea. We should go talk to Elizabeth. Maybe borrow some of T.K.'s clothes."

Frank spotted Tommy, already on his way back, and his shoulders slumped. "Looks like he got breakfast from T.K.'s garage."

Tommy approached and lowered a six pack of beer to the ground at their feet. He pointed at the green plastic sheeting beneath them. "Hey, give me my rain slicker."

Mac pulled another modified trash bag from under him and handed it to Tommy.

Frank jerked a beer from the six pack and held it up for Tommy to see. "I was thinking more like a *donut*."

Tommy shrugged. "Beer's the same thing. It's liquid bread."

Frank decided it wouldn't be wise to deal with the marauders while wearing his uniform and smelling of beer, particularly at seven o'clock in the morning. He put down his unopened beer. Tommy and Mac drank their breakfast and appreciated the wonder of T.K.'s final home improvement project. Three weeks before he died, tired of being bedridden and confined to a life of afternoon talk shows, T.K. had dragged the bombs he'd collected as a child out of the garage. The yellow-grey dummies now stood like sentries around his smallest tomato field, closest to his house. Four coveted dud silver bombs marked the corners. Spaced much too far apart to be useful, the bomb fence wouldn't stop furry pests unless they happened to be a marauding band of tomato-eating cattle, but they added a feeling of *security* to the crop.

For a man with T.K.'s advanced case of lung cancer, building a bomb fence proved to be a poor sort of relaxation. Elizabeth returned from the food store that fateful day to find him collapsed on his compost heap, dead.

Tommy pulled a candy bar from his jacket pocket and picked the fuzzies from its half-eaten end. "We gotta get a plan rollin' here."

Frank's stomach growled. "We'll talk to that bastard when he gets here, tell him we need time to go over the papers. I'll call the judge at eight and get him to stop this."

"What if they don't listen?" asked Mac.

"All we can do—" Frank's gaze settled on Tommy's candy bar. "What is *that*?"

"Candy bar. I had it in my jacket. Want some?"

Frank grimaced. "No."

Mac looked as if he was about to snatch the candy from Tommy, but then he cocked his head. "Hey, you hear something?"

The low grumble Frank thought was his stomach grew louder. He stood. Beyond the field, he saw dust rising from the road.

He hung his thumbs behind his soggy belt. "Here they come."

CHAPTER NINE

Angelina walked into the room on the tenth and uppermost floor of the Loggerhead Inn, her teacup Yorkshire terrier, Harley, tucked in the crook of her elbow. She nodded to the nurse sitting in a padded chair in the corner of the suite.

"I've got him for a bit," she said.

The nurse gathered the book she'd been reading without a word and left. Angelina moved to the door separating the sitting room from the adjoining bedroom and rapped on it.

"Mick, it's Angelina. I'm coming in. Pull up your pants."

She always said that. It was their thing.

She opened the door. In a hospital-style bed, a salt-and-pepper-haired man lay still, his eyes closed, arms at his side. Chrome safety bars rose on either side of him to keep him from falling out of bed during one of his occasional seizures. Light filtered through the thin orange draperies, giving the room a strange after-the-bomb yellow glow.

But it sort of is the end of the world for you, isn't it, Mick?

Surprised to be caught off guard by Mick's stillness *again*, Angelina opened the drapes to let in more natural light and cracked open the window. January in South Florida had the winter breezes picking up, and the air cooled the skin instead of just pushing the humidity back and forth. Angelina knew Mick liked the smell of the outdoors. If he were dreaming, somewhere in that locked skull of his, it might be nice for him to believe he was outside, where he belonged.

She sat in a wicker chair beside the bed, shifting when a cracked piece of cane poked at her spine. Months of the nurse and herself sitting, standing, and sitting again had turned the relatively new chair shabby-chic before its time. She made a mental note to get a new one. Something more sturdy yet comfortable.

"How are you doing today, sport?" she asked, patting his hand.

He didn't answer. She wasn't surprised.

"Good. Me too. Same as always. Except for one thing. I think there's someone downstairs looking for Siofra." She paused and smiled. "I know. Who isn't looking for her, right? I'm just not sure what to tell her. Tell the young lady that is not Siofra. Do you want me to tell her the truth?"

Angelina placed Harley on Mick's chest, and the little dog circled twice before lying down. Angelina continued.

"She says she has a picture, and the call came from Charity, Florida, over on the other side. You know the place. I saw her as she was coming in. Just a glimpse, but she looks like—" She grimaced.

He doesn't need to know that yet.

"It's all pretty weird," she said instead.

Angelina figure-eighted the tip of her index finger between his knuckles. His permanent tan had faded. Age spots had grown more prominent. His skin felt crêpey, so she added another item to her mental list.

Moisturize his hands more often.

"Ah, Mickey. I wish you were here."

Angelina laid her head on his chest beside Harley, letting her head rise and fall with his breathing. The dog stood and licked her forehead once before pouncing on her face. She sat up and tucked the dog back into her crooked elbow.

"I guess I'll play it by ear. Right?"

She stood and offered Mick a close-lipped smile. A trail of

tears drew shiny lines from the corners of his eyes, making it look like he was crying. On the side of his head closest to her, she traced the wide scar that never lost its angry red glow. It traveled five inches above his ear and arced around to the back of his shaved head. A network of blue vein roadways ran in every direction beneath his thinning skin.

She patted his hand again. "I'm glad we had this little talk. You always know what to do. You always did."

Angelina exited the room and entered the main living area just as the nurse returned. She pointed back to the bedroom. "Thanks, Martisha. Can you be sure to moisturize his hands? They're looking a little dry."

Martisha nodded, and Angelina headed back downstairs to the lobby.

Time to talk to Charlotte.

CHAPTER TEN

"Sonuva—"

Standing in Mariska's foyer with Abby and Izzy on leashes beside him, Declan jumped at the sound of the voice. He turned to find Bob walking through the door.

"Hey, Bob."

Bob looked up, seeming equally as surprised to see him. "What are you doing here?" he looked down and pointed. "That's my dog."

Declan chuckled. "Yep. Charlotte went out of town, and she left Abby with Mariska. Remember?"

Bob grunted.

Declan paused until he realized that was all the answer he would get. "I thought I'd swing by and walk the dogs before heading home."

"It's late."

"I closed up the shop and did bills for a bit. Catching up."

"Good, good." Bob sighed.

"Something wrong?"

"Aah." He waved his hand through the air as if swatting at a fly. "Some guy came to the bar talking about T.K."

"What's T.K.?"

"Not *what's. Who*. The Tomato King."

Declan recalled the sign touting the freshness of the tomatoes of The Tomato King. He'd passed it a million times over the years. "Oh, that farm out there off three-oh-one?"

Bob nodded. "He died. T.K. Couple of weeks ago."

"You knew him?"

"He was a Gopher."

"Your drinking group?"

"It's a *lodge*."

"Right. Drinking group." Declan grinned.

Bob tried not to, but the corner of his mouth curled up for one brief second, and he leaned forward to take Izzy's leash. "Give me my dog, you smartass."

Declan laughed and handed him both leashes before leaning down to unclip them. The dogs had already sensed they were in for a story and sat down.

"So you said someone came in looking for T.K.?"

"Yeah. Looking to serve him papers, kicking him off his land."

"Yikes."

"Yeah, yikes. His wife, Elizabeth, is still there. Tommy, Mac, and Frank went there to see if they could help."

"And you feel bad you didn't go?"

He nodded. "I was already late. Mariska would have—"

As if invoked, Mariska appeared from the lanai.

"What are you two doing? It's late. Let the boy go home, Bob."

Bob grunted.

"They both did their thing," said Declan, motioning to the dogs.

"Thank you." Mariska's gaze returned to Bob. "He saw me struggling out there trying to walk two dogs and helped out. *You* were too busy out drinking."

"There was an emergency," said Bob, not looking at her.

She scoffed. "Emergency need for a drink."

"*No*, someone's trying to kick T.K. off his land."

"T.K.'s dead."

"Kick Elizabeth off then, you know what I mean."

Mariska put her hands on her hips. "Well, that makes more sense now."

"What does?"

"Frank called Darla, and Darla called me. He told her to tell me to tell *you* to meet them at T.K.'s in the morning. They're staying overnight to keep watch. I didn't get why then, but now it makes more sense."

Bob nodded. "Okay. Will do. You can send it back up the wire that I'll be there."

"You can send it yourself. Who was that who brought you home?"

"Herbert. He was going to watch *House Hunters* with me, but he changed his mind."

"Lucky for you." Mariska headed down the hall toward the bedroom. "Come on, dogs."

The dogs stood and trotted after her.

"Sounds like you're literally in the dog house," said Declan to Bob as she walked away.

Bob frowned. "You *are* a smartass. Hey, you wanna come?"

"Where? The Tomato Farm?"

"Sure. Why not? You working tomorrow?"

"Not until four."

"Okay. Come pick me up. You can help us protest."

Declan smiled. Bob had recently stopped driving due to a small problem with his heart, which resulted in low blood pressure in his brain and the occasional fainting spell. Or, more correctly, Mariska had *informed* him he wouldn't be driving until he got his pacemaker. She didn't want him nodding off at the wheel.

Bob hated spending the money on cabs, so Declan had a good idea why he'd been invited to join.

"Don't think Mariska will drive you to the farm to protest with your buddies?"

He frowned. "Not a chance. Come on. It'll be fun. There'll be beer."

Declan laughed. "Sure. Wouldn't miss it. What time?"

"Like seven?"

"In the morning?"

He nodded.

Declan looked at his watch.

So much for sleeping in.

"Sure. See you at seven."

Bob nodded and started back up the hallway. "I'd like to be there at seven, so come early."

Declan nodded. "Sure."

CHAPTER ELEVEN

Charlotte opened the door to her hotel room and stood at the entry, admiring it.

So cute.

Crisp white sheets peeked out from beneath a coral-patterned quilt. Sea-turtle-themed art graced all the available surfaces, each item perfectly treading the line between art and Florida kitsch. A canvas painting of an orange sunrise peeking between the pilings of a tall pier hung on the wall above the bed, surf crashing in the foreground.

Beach-themed rooms usually leaned towards tacky, but whoever decorated her room had taste. Charlotte was impressed, and a feeling of well-being settled over her. All thoughts of her odd experiences downstairs washed away with the surf in the painting.

Charlotte tossed her duffle bag on the luggage stand and frowned at it.

The room was too nice for a duffle bag.

I need to upgrade my luggage.

She took a few minutes to lay out her bathroom things and freshen up. Feeling as if she'd been given a chance to start the day anew, she stood by the window and gazed down at the gently flowing waters of the Intracoastal Waterway. The sizeable lawn below separated the hotel from the water, where several boats sat docked at each of three piers. A pelican perched on one of the pilings trying to choke back a fish as big as its head.

Charlotte took a deep breath and released it slowly. She took a photo with her phone and texted it to Declan before slipping the device into the pouch of her thin hoodie.

Let's do this.

She spun on her heel and headed back downstairs, hoping the concierge had returned to her station at the desk.

What was her name again? Something sort of sexy and exotic-sounding...

Angelina.

Sounded like a World War II Italian femme fatale. She hadn't looked that old, though. Maybe early sixties.

If Angelina wasn't there, Charlotte decided she'd get some food and then hope to bump into her on her return. If she intentionally avoided her, she wouldn't be able to hide all day.

Charlotte was still thinking about the pelican on the piling and its chances of swallowing that enormous fish when the elevator doors opened, and she found herself staring at the back of a woman's head.

Dark hair. Sitting in the concierge's seat.

Helloooo, Angelina.

She strode out of the elevator and, after a passing urge to park herself behind the chair so Angelina couldn't scurry away again, stationed herself at the front of the desk like a normal human being. A tiny Yorkie sleeping in a faux-fur bed on the corner of the desk rose to its feet. The woman put her hand on the dog's butt to hold it in place and looked up at her, smiling with bright white teeth. The dog and the grin melted away any irritation Charlotte might have harbored.

How could someone with that dog and that smile be up to no good?

High cheekbones, full lips, stormy blue eyes—Angelina had all the hallmarks of an aging beauty. Undoubtedly, she was the knockout in the photograph she'd admitted to being on the phone.

Charlotte assumed Angelina lived and worked in Florida full time, but she wore dark tights and red boots with a V-neck black sweater that did an admirable job of promoting her cleavage. The outfit seemed wintery for the Sunshine State in any season, but as a fellow Floridian, Charlotte knew the locals' blood tended to run thin. Fifty-five degrees in Florida was like sub-zero in other parts of the country. She guessed, though, that the woman had originally come from a chillier clime and never lost her love of black clothing.

"Can I help you?" Angelina asked, her expression open and genuine. She looked as if nothing would make her happier than recommending a nice place to eat lunch.

If only it were that easy.

"Hi. Are you Angelina?"

"Last time I checked."

Though the answer could be filed under *smartass*, the smile, again, made it impossible to receive the line as anything other than playful.

"Who's your friend?" Charlotte motioned to the dog. The Yorkie had sat beneath the weight of her mother's insistence, but she stomped her front paws to show her *need* to say *hi*.

"This is Harley." Angelina gave up holding the dog in place and trotted across the desk to get pets from Charlotte. When the love-fest ended, the Yorkie returned to her bed, and Charlotte pulled the newspaper clipping she'd found in the attic shoebox from her pocket. She unfolded it and pointed to Angelina in the photo.

"Is this you?" she asked.

"Oh, look at *me*," said Angelina, resting her chin on her hand. "I loved that shirt. I wonder what I did with that?"

Angelina beamed at the photo with such longing Charlotte found *herself* wondering what the woman might have done with the pretty blouse in the picture before pulling her mind back to the task at hand.

Time to get to work.

"I'm Charlotte Morgan. I called asking about Siofra?"

"Mm." Angelina's grunt rang neither positive nor negative. She remained, staring at the photo.

"Is this her?" Charlotte moved her finger to another beauty, this one younger and unsmiling. Her eyes weren't on the camera but looking at something to the photographer's left. "Or maybe this?" she moved to another woman in the photo about the same age. This one was blonde and smiling. Chipmunk cheeks humped beneath her eyes.

Angelina looked up at her and licked her lower lip. "I'm sorry, I forgot your name."

"Charlotte Morgan."

"Morgan. That's a nice last name. Like Captain Morgan. Are you heir to the Captain Morgan fortune? Can you get me a discount?" Angelina laughed.

Is she purposely trying to dodge my question?

Charlotte forced a chuckle. "Different branch of the family, I'm afraid."

Angelina shrugged. "That's okay. I don't drink rum anyway. I might switch if you gave me a discount, though."

Charlotte waited a moment, hoping the silence would start Angelina talking.

I'm not going to forget what I asked you.

Angelina's expression shifted as if she'd heard Charlotte's inner dialog. "Where did you get this picture? It's old."

"I found it in a box in my grandmother's attic."

"Really? She maybe stayed here? Kept it for her scrapbook?"

"Maybe. But everything else in the box was about a girl named Siofra. I couldn't help but think *she* was one of the people in this photo."

"Your grandmother?"

"No. *Siofra*."

Angelina grimaced. "Hm. I'm embarrassed to say I haven't

had a chance to ask around about a Siofra since you called. I apologize. Right after I got your call, some things came up— small emergency in the kitchen—you know how it goes. I wasn't expecting you to stop by."

"I had to come over here on business anyway." Charlotte swallowed.

Why did I lie?

"Oh? What do you do?" asked Angelina.

Crap. Now she takes an interest. Figures.

Charlotte said the first thing that came to her mind.

"Health Inspector."

She did her best not to cringe. Angelina had just mentioned the kitchen, which triggered her brain to say she was a health inspector. Maybe she wanted to intimidate Angelina a little. The woman knew something. She could feel it.

Angelina laughed. "Uh oh. Are we in trouble?"

"No, I'm here for a conference."

"In Jupiter Beach?"

Charlotte nodded.

I have to get off this topic before I dig this hole any deeper.

"Do you know any good places in town to eat? I should grab some lunch before, uh, my meetings. I guess you have a restaurant here?"

"Would I tell you if we did?" Angelina winked.

She actually *winked*.

The effect would have been cheesy and off-putting on any other person, but somehow, it only endeared Angelina to Charlotte.

What is it with this woman? She's like a siren.

"Just kidding," continued Angelina. "We've got nothing to fear. For one, we don't have a restaurant—just light room service and bar snacks. But if you'd like to go out, I have a list of different places that offer lunch here." Angelina opened a drawer and pulled out half a white sheet of paper to hand to her. A list of restaurants and their cuisine type lined the page, printed in a large font for easy reading.

"Great." Charlotte let her eye run over the list as if it was absorbing. "I'll go grab something to eat. In the meantime—"

"I'll see what I can find out for you," finished Angelina.

"That would be great. Thank you."

"Mind if I keep the photo to show around?"

Charlotte glanced at the newspaper clipping. It was the only evidence she had of her mystery aunt, and she felt protective of it. On the other hand, it would be unreasonable to ask Angelina to ask around about the photo *without the photo.*

"Didn't you say you had a copy?"

Angelina seemed amused. "I do. Somewhere. But it would take me to find it the entire time you're gone. I'm not what you'd call an *organized* person."

Charlotte shifted, trying to keep herself from snatching up the photo.

Somehow, I think you're a very organized person.

Her fingers twitched, but she found a way to stop the urge.

Let it go. No reason this woman would steal the photo.

"Okay. Sure. Of course you can keep it. I'll see you when I get back?"

"I'll be here." Angelina stood and moved in front of the desk. She draped her arm over Charlotte's shoulder, nudging her forward to walk her toward the front door.

"I'll find someone who remembers something about this photo. We have a very loyal staff. Many of them have been here since the beginning."

Behind them, Harley yipped once, obviously to show her annoyance at being abandoned.

"That's great. The, uh, rooms are adorable," said Charlotte, unable to think of anything else.

"Thank you. We aim to please."

Angelina tripped on her high heel boot, and Charlotte shifted her weight to catch her.

"Are you okay?"

Angelina laughed. "Old wooden floors. Little lumpy." She patted Charlotte's back hard enough to come just short of pushing her toward the door. "I'll see you soon."

Charlotte nodded and left the hotel.

"Crabgrass kittens," said the doorman, tipping his hat.

She turned. "Thank you."

He smiled.

"Stuffing."

Charlotte strode to her car and sat inside with her hands on the wheel until the first bead of sweat dripped from her hairline. She'd parked in the sun, so it only took about two seconds.

Did she trip on purpose to make me catch her? To make me care about her?

She put her key into the Volvo and turned up the air-conditioning.

I think I'm going crazy.

CHAPTER TWELVE

Angelina watched Charlotte leave the resort. Once the old Volvo had crunched out of the stone parking lot, she stood and scurried over to Croix, who'd been watching their interaction and trying hard to pretend she wasn't.

Harley barked again.

"Shush it." Angelina handed Croix Charlotte's phone. "Open."

Croix smiled at the stolen item.

"Nice move."

She took the phone and stepped into the back. When she returned, she had a black gadget in her hand, which she plugged into the bottom of the phone. A minute later, she handed the phone back to Angelina, unlocked.

"Ta da."

Angelina flipped through the device.

"Boyfriend, I'm guessing," she said, holding up the phone so Croix could see the picture of a young man in swimming trunks on the screen.

Croix's eyebrows raised. "Wow. Hottie."

Angelina nodded and scrolled through some text threads. "Not too shabby. Declan. Nice Irish name. She's got a dog, Abby. Mariska. Mother? Maybe. What was the passcode?"

"You just said it."

Angelina looked up. "What?"

"One, two, two, twenty-five."

She cocked her head. "Twenty-five?"

"A-B-B-Y. One for A, Two for B, Y is twenty-five."

"Ah. Remind me I need to teach you to count cards. We're going to make a fortune."

Croix giggled.

Angelina crooked her finger, beckoning to the girl with a long, crimson-painted nail. "I need everything you have on her."

"I have her room key."

"Big deal. I have the master key. What about her credit card?"

"I told her we trusted her."

Angelina rolled her eyes. "You have to stop doing that. We can't trust *everyone*. It's a business."

"Yeah, yeah. But half the people here—"

"I check *them* in personally. Don't I?"

"Yes."

"You check in the civilians. *Those* people need to give us a credit card."

"Got it." Croix looked crestfallen and then perked. "Look at the back of the phone."

Angelina flipped over the phone and saw the edge of a plastic card peeking out from a slit in the leather. She pulled it out and frowned.

"It's her credit card. She won't be able to pay for lunch and will notice her phone is missing. Don't you people ever carry purses anymore?"

"Not if I can help it," muttered Croix. She tapped on the keyboard of her computer. "I have her license plate number on the check-in card."

"That's something. Give me that."

Croix found the card Charlotte had filled out upon checking in and handed it to Angelina, who scanned over the info. She strolled to the desk to retrieve her pet and hand the Yorkie to Croix. Slipping Charlotte's phone into her pocket, she headed toward the elevator.

On the fourth floor, she used her master key on room four eleven. She watched a boat roll by from inside the French doors that led to the balcony and then turned to observe the rest of the room.

Let's start with the bathroom.

Items arranged neatly on the counter.

Splashing in the sink.

Nothing in the trashcan.

Nothing in the closet.

Angelina moved back into the tiny hall separating the bathroom from the bedroom. She gave the handle of the room safe a tug.

Safe locked.

She hovered near the safe a moment longer and then moved back into the main room.

Easy stuff next.

Her eye fell on the duffle bag she'd seen the girl yank out of her car and frowned, slightly offended.

This isn't a roadside motel.

She unzipped the bag and rustled through the sparse clothing inside. A couple of shirts, pair of shorts, and what looked like a sleeping shirt.

Angelina sniffed.

Meeting, my ass.

The bag didn't hold a single item of clothing someone could wear to a health inspector's meeting.

Patting the hidden front pouch of her sweater, Angelina found the card Croix had given her and pulled Charlotte's phone from her pocket to dial.

"Hey, Artie, how are you?" she purred when a man's voice answered. On the other side of the line, it sounded as if Officer Artie Janket had choked on a French fry, which he *had* if Angelina had to lay down money.

"Miss Angelina," he sputtered between gagging noises. He

took a moment to catch his breath and then returned to the conversation. "To what do I owe this great pleasure?"

"I need a peek at a license."

"Aw, Angelina. You know I'm not supposed to do that sort of thing."

"Artie, if you don't, I'll find someone who will."

He sighed. "I suppose that's true enough. Hit me with it."

She rattled off the plate number.

"Got it. Charlotte Morgan. Driving a Volvo 240 wagon. No outstanding warrants. No arrests. Hm."

"What, *hm*?"

"Says she's a licensed private detective."

"Her?"

"That's what it says."

Angelina felt her stomach gurgle.

I need to eat something.

She moved to Charlotte's mini bar and pulled out a tiny vodka. She cracked the top and took a sip.

"What was that?" asked Artie.

"Cracking my knuckles. Anything else?"

"No. She's clean."

"Address? I have one here. Can I check it against that?"

"Sure."

She read off the address, and Artie grunted an affirmative. "That's it."

"Thanks. You're a doll."

"You free for dinner this week?"

"I might be. Can I get back to you?"

"Of course you can, darlin'. I'd wait until the full moon comes back for you."

"That's tomorrow."

"Then the next one."

"Gotcha. Talk to you later. Thanks again, Artie."

She hung up, deleted the call from the phone, and thought for a second, pulling at her earring.

Time for the safe.

She moved to the guest room safe and plugged in her override sequence. Inside sat a laptop computer and a shoe box.

A shoebox? Why would a girl with a duffle bag for a suitcase bring shoes so nice she needs to keep them in the box?

Khaki shorts and Louboutins.

Nope.

Angelina pulled out the box and flipped open the lid. Inside were papers of every size and color. A child's drawing on pink construction paper, a page of math problems with a circled red A, and report cards with the name Siofra on them.

Angelina swallowed.

The last names scrawled on the school papers varied. Siofra Candish. Siofra Foxtrot. Siofra Blake. But the first name was always the same. *Siofra.* Even one of the child's drawings had the name Siofra on it.

Angelina sat on the bed.

This isn't good.

What other information might this Charlotte have? Who is she?

The ironic part was she kind of *looked* like Siofra. The last time she saw her, anyway. It had been a while. And even then, she wasn't *Siofra.* She was Lily.

Who knew who she was now?

Angelina took another sip from the vodka bottle and returned to the safe to slide out the computer. She opened the lid and stared at the password box.

Locked, of course.

Croix had taught her a couple of ways to break into a laptop, but after doing so, she'd have to reset the password, which would give her away.

What was the dog's name?

Abby. One-Two-Two-Twenty-five.

She plugged in the numbers, and the screen shook but didn't switch to the desktop.

Shoot.

She thought about a few other possibilities and decided to start simple.

Let's give it a shot.

She typed in a-b-b-y.

The computer sprang to life.

People are so predictable.

She poked around and found notes from other cases the girl detective had worked. There was a lot of information about a girl named Stephanie Moriarty. Angelina made a note to remember that name. Most of the crimes looked small time. Nothing too sinister, except some notes implying ole Stephanie might be a serial killer.

That's interesting.

But not relevant.

She opened a browser and visited a real estate site to look up Charlotte's address. She owned the house she lived in. Last owned by Estelle—

Angelina's face went tingly.

Last owned by Mick's ex-wife.

This girl was a private detective living in the home of Siofra's mother.

Oh this is not good.

Angelina slapped the computer closed and slipped it back into the safe. She returned the shoebox and locked the safe door.

She tidied—zipped shut the duffle bag, tucked the fun-sized vodka into her pocket, fluffed up the spot on the bed where'd she sat, and with a final sweeping glance of the area, left.

Once downstairs, she hustled out the front door.

"Where you going?" called Croix as she hustled by.

Angelina waved her away. "No time."

As she approached, the doorman opened the door, and she stopped to put a hand on his chest.

"Which way did she go?"

"Basket stop." He pointed to the left.

"What do you think? Sushi?"

He squinted and then nodded.

She patted him on the chest. "I think so too. Thanks, Bracco."

He smiled, and she hurried for her car. It wouldn't be long until the girl realized her phone was missing and needed to be there to save the day.

CHAPTER THIRTEEN

"Hey, fancy meeting you here."

Charlotte looked up from her sushi roll to find Angelina from the Loggerhead Inn walking towards her. Striding as if she were late for a lunch date. The woman bristled with confidence.

What is going on with this lady? She'd practically pushed her out of the hotel, and now she was here as if she couldn't get enough of her.

"Hello again. I guess that's why this place is on your list?" said Charlotte as Angelina arrived tableside.

"Hm?" Angelina cocked her head and looked at the ground through one eye like a bird.

"Your list. I guess this place is on it because *you* like it."

"Oh right. Sure." She stooped, disappearing below the table, and then popped up again with a familiar item in her hand. "Is this your phone?"

Charlotte patted the pouch of her hoodie where she'd last put the phone. "Yikes. Yes. Thank you. How did that fall?" She took the phone and slipped it back into its home. Thank goodness Angelina *had* come along. She would have panicked if she'd reached to find her phone and found it missing.

Uninvited, Angelina sat at Charlotte's small, round, high-top table and began shifting the centerpiece and a spare set of silverware as if they were chess pieces, clearing a sight path to Charlotte on the opposite side of the table. "So, tell me more about why you're looking for Siofra?" she said.

Charlotte's mouth hung open a crack, her brain unable to unlock.

Why is this woman here?

She decided there was nothing left to do but play along. "I think she was important to my grandmother."

"And who was your grandmother?"

Charlotte frowned. Every interaction with the woman felt one-sided. She didn't like that suddenly Angelina got to ask all the questions.

"Does this mean you figured out who Siofra is?" she asked.

Angelina ignored her and instead raised a hand to flag down a waitress. When the server shifted directions and moved to the table, Angelina smiled.

"Is this your table, Susan?"

The server grinned and nodded. It was clear to Charlotte she was happy to see Angelina.

"Great. Sweetheart, could you get me a Clamato and vodka?"

Susan nodded and continued on her way.

Angelina refocused on Charlotte and leaned in as if she were sharing a secret. "They hate it when you ask them for something, and it isn't their table."

Charlotte nodded.

Angelina continued. "I don't usually drink this early, but my nerves are shot—"

"Why?"

"Why don't I drink this early?"

"Why are your nerves shot?"

Angelina shrugged. "Oh. It's Tuesday. What were we talking about? I think you were about to tell me who your grandmother is in relation to Siofra?"

Charlotte frowned.

She's got the upper hand again. How did that happen?

"No, I asked *you* if you figured out who Siofra is," she said.

"Oh. Right. *Maybe*. I just want to narrow things down a bit."

"I don't understand."

Angelina turned a palm to the sky. Her fingers splayed out like ruby-tipped peacock feathers. "I mean, I can't just *give* you the names and addresses of everyone who worked at the resort. I have to find out *why* you want to know. You could be a debt collector, for all I know."

"But I'm a food inspector." Charlotte felt like an idiot repeating her stupid lie but had to stick with her cover.

Wait, did I say health inspector or food inspector the first time?

She wasn't sure.

Shoot.

Angelina nodded. "So you say. But that's something a debt collector might say, isn't it?"

"And knowing who my grandmother is would tell you if I'm a debt collector?"

Angelina shrugged. "Maybe."

Charlotte took a deep breath. "Okay. Fine. It seems neither of us wants to be the first to share, and we're going around in circles. Let's start over."

"Fine." Angelina studied her nails. "I don't know why you wouldn't trust *me*. You're a *health* inspector who showed up asking for information. I have reason to be afraid of you."

"Why? Is your kitchen in violation?"

"No. But you know how *health* inspectors are."

Charlotte couldn't miss the emphasis Angelina placed on the word "health," now certain the woman had caught her mistake.

I said health inspector the first time. Not food inspector.

A close-lipped smile seeped onto Angelina's face, and Charlotte knew one other thing: Angelina hadn't believed she was a health or food inspector for a *minute*.

I could admit I lied or push it.

"Why did you say *health inspector* like that?" she asked.

Angelina's eyes grew wide. "Like what?"

"Like you don't believe I am one."

"Well, you're not, are you?"

"Why would you say that?"

"Because nothing about you says health inspector. Health inspectors are always chubby old men."

"That's not true."

Angelina pointed at her. "You're not dressed like a government employee."

"We have days off, too, you know."

"You said you were here for a *meeting.* And if you weren't, somehow I doubt health inspectors get so intrigued by family mysteries they run to the other side of the state to figure them out."

Charlotte scowled. "You seem to have an awful lot of preconceived notions about health inspectors."

"Oh, I'm sorry. I don't want to miss it. Where are they holding your meeting again? Sounds like a *party.* And is it the health inspector meeting or the *food* inspector meeting? I keep forgetting."

Charlotte frowned.

I knew it was a stupid lie.

Her shoulders slumped. "Fine. I'm not a health inspector. But my stupid little fib would have worked if you hadn't been so suspicious."

"Touché. But why did you feel the need to lie?"

"Because I thought if I told you my real job, it would make you suspicious."

"Right. We wouldn't want that."

Charlotte snorted a laugh. "Why *are* you being so dodgy about sharing information?"

"I'm not being *dodgy.* I'm a concierge. Not a spy. I just don't know what's going on."

"Fair enough." It occurred to Charlotte that Angelina hadn't asked her what her *real* profession was. Strange for a woman who'd been so suspicious of her.

Almost as if she already knows.

Angelina's cheek twitched as if, beneath Charlotte's glare, she'd realized her mistake.

Looking away as if the answer would have no importance to her, Angelina asked the question.

"So what are you? A cop?"

Without meaning to, a tiny grunt escaped from Charlotte's throat.

There it is. She's covering. She realized she should have asked. This woman is good.

Charlotte decided to come clean, so they wouldn't spend the next day playing cat and mouse. "No. Not a cop. A private detective."

Angelina seemed shocked. "Really?"

She nodded.

"Isn't that interesting?"

"Sometimes."

Susan delivered Angelina's drink and wandered off again. Angelina plucked out the cocktail straw and sipped the thick, red-tomato-juice-based concoction.

"The salt makes me bloat, but I love these things," she said before returning her attention to Charlotte. "So what else did you find at Grandmom's, Sherlock?"

Charlotte chuckled. "A shoebox full of a mishmash of kid things, mostly. Report cards, drawings—made me think this girl must have been special to Nanny."

"That's what you called your grandmother? Nanny?"

She nodded.

Angelina looked off into the restaurant as if a memory pulled her thoughts in that direction.

"Mine was Nona." Her shoulders seemed to loosen like the tight strings holding her erect had slipped a notch. "Siofra's been gone a long time."

Bingo!

Charlotte perked. "So you *do* know her?"

She nodded. "She's been missing for years."

"Missing? Like, kidnapped?"

"Gosh, no, I hope not. She just left. Personal reasons. We made some inquiries but nothing solid. Until recently, we didn't know if she wanted to be found, so we didn't try."

"What happened recently?"

"Her father fell ill. We want to let her know, but I'm afraid her trail has been cold for too long."

"Are you family?"

Angelina tilted her head from side to side. "Family friend."

Charlotte ate a piece of her sushi roll.

Declan was right. This wasn't going to be a one-day project.

Dabbing her napkin against her lip, she stared across the table. "I'm looking for her anyway. Do you want me to do it for you?"

Angelina's brow creased. "You mean, do I want to *hire* you?"

"No, I'd do it for free, but yes, find her like I would if you *were to* hire me."

Angelina took another sip of her Clamato and vodka and mumbled to herself, bouncing her knuckle on her lip as if weighing the pros and cons. She began to nod, the motion growing stronger until she put down her glass and locked eyes with Charlotte.

"I think I can give you some leads, Sherlock."

CHAPTER FOURTEEN

Charlotte gobbled the last few pieces of her sushi, settled the bill, and followed Angelina back to the resort. She paid for Angelina's cocktail as a thank you for recovering her phone, and Angelina accepted without a fight.

"Cattle cup," said the doorman touching the brim of his invisible cap as he opened the door for them.

Angelina strode through without stopping. "Thank you, Bracco."

Charlotte smiled and hurried to catch up to Angelina. Flanking the concierge, she lowered her voice to a whisper.

"Is it me, or is he not saying real sentences?"

She felt bad for asking, but it was time to figure out if she was going crazy or if that man was saying random words every time she passed by.

"They're real sentences. They just don't make any sense to *us*." Angelina tapped the side of her head with her index finger. "Brain injury. He knows what he's saying, but his brain and mouth aren't on speaking terms."

"Oh."

"A lot of the people who work here are veterans or survivors of other types of wars."

Charlotte glanced back at the tattoo-covered body of Croix at the desk, wondering which war she'd survived. Croix smiled and offered her a tiny wave.

Angelina led Charlotte away from the reception area and turned her back as she punched a code into the lock of a door at the end of a long hallway. Charlotte noted they'd moved in the same direction Angelina had disappeared upon her arrival at the Inn. Though the room didn't use a key card like hers, inside, it looked very much the same, but for the mess. It was clear housekeeping had been told to skip that room and that maybe Angelina wasn't lying when she confessed to being unorganized.

"Do you live here?" asked Charlotte.

Angelina grabbed the crumpled sheets at the bottom of the bed and flung them towards the pillows at the head in what looked like a half-hearted attempt to make it. "Sometimes."

The door clicked shut behind them, and Charlotte turned to find several extra bolt locks. She didn't have to look far before she spotted a long thin piece of metal leaning against the wall. Upward-pointing square hooks hung on either side of the door, looking very much like the sort of hooks someone would place a large piece of wood or metal into to brace a door. She suspected it fit perfectly between those two hooks.

Charlotte motioned to the locks. "Should I be worried?"

"Hm?" Angelina made another lackluster attempt to make the bed and then shooed at it as if it could get up and leave in shame.

"Expecting someone?" Charlotte added, still pointing at the multitude of locks.

"Always," said Angelina without looking up. She opened bureau drawers, one after the next, rifling through balled-up clothing until she pulled out a small wooden box. She carried it to the bed and opened it to retrieve a wad of postcards from inside. "These are from her."

She handed them to Charlotte, who sat on the most-made corner of the bed to study the cards, flipping over one after the next. Each was from a different state and town, but none had any writing on them except the address of the Loggerhead Inn.

"How do you know they're from her?" she asked.

Angelina looked grim. "I know."

"Is there a reason she'd send blank cards?"

"To let her father know she's alive—" Angelina looked away, and Charlotte suspected she'd said more than she'd meant to.

"Her *father* is alive? He's here?"

"Would that be strange?"

"It would mean you've always known more about her than you were letting on."

Angelina's expression fell slack, losing all readability. "Not necessarily."

Charlotte frowned. She wasn't in the mood to fall into the rabbit hole of Angelina's pathological subterfuge. "My grandfather died the same year Siofra was born. I figured the last thing he did—"

Angelina laughed. "Was knock up your grandmother?"

"Yes. But the name on the birth certificate—"

"Wasn't your grandfather's name."

"No. I thought maybe it was altered for a reason I couldn't know." She squinted at Angelina. "You're saying my grandmother had Siofra with another man? And he's *here*?"

Angelina nodded. "He owns the place."

"But he's *here*?"

Angelina fiddled with some invisible thing in her hand and mumbled her answer. "In the penthouse."

Charlotte looked up as if she could teleport her way to the top of the building. There was something odd about the way Angelina seemed to know, without a doubt, he was in the penthouse at *that moment*. "Can I talk to him?"

"That would be difficult."

"Why?"

"He's in a coma."

"Oh."

That explains that.

"Can I ask what happened?"

Angelina stiffened. "No." She looked away and then looked back, her expression softening. "Not yet. Maybe later."

"You understand that makes Siofra my aunt?"

Angelina nodded. "Half-aunt. Why do you think I told you about Mick?"

"You mean *Shea*?"

Angelina tilted her head and smiled at her as if she pitied her for her slow-moving brain. "Nickname. Think about it."

By then, Charlotte had already worked it out.

McQueen. Mick. Right.

She flipped through the postcards again, sorting them in order of postmark. The dates were widely spaced, often six months or more apart.

"Does Mick know about these? Did the locations mean anything to him?"

"He knew about a few before..." She flicked her hand in the air to invoke whatever had happened to the man.

Charlotte searched for any kind of pattern. "Is there any reason to believe there might be significance to the locations?"

Angelina shrugged one shoulder. "Maybe. Mick's good at codes." She scratched the back of her head. "Among other things."

"What do you mean *he's good at codes*?"

"I didn't mean anything by it. He just is."

"You mean, like, for the NSA?"

Angelina stared at her until she looked away.

Okay. Not answering that one.

Charlotte huffed. "We'll come back to that." She lifted the wad of postcards. "But you're saying there may be a pattern here? Not crazy to think there might be a hint?"

"Not crazy. Though I can tell you, I haven't figured it out."

"And he didn't either?"

"Not that he mentioned."

Charlotte took a deep breath, struck again by the idea that

her grandmother had a child with a man who might be a few hundred feet away from her. Did her mother ever know she had a sister?

"What is it?" asked Angelina.

Charlotte snapped from her thoughts. "Huh? Oh. Nothing. I thought that my Nanny found a new man fast after my grandfather died."

Angelina laughed. "*Old* man."

Charlotte scowled. "He's old?"

"No, well *yes*, but not then. That's not what I meant. There's something else you should probably know."

Charlotte found herself worried by the woman's suddenly serious tone. "What?"

"By *old*, I meant it wasn't the first time."

Charlotte blinked. "What wasn't the first time?"

"It wasn't the first time Mick and Estelle had a child."

Charlotte's jaw fell open. "You mean *my mother*?"

Angelina pressed her lips together and nodded.

"That would make Mick—"

"Your real grandfather, too. They were married. Briefly."

"So Siofra's my *full* aunt? One hundred percent? You knew this all along?"

"Sort of."

"Why didn't you say?"

"Why do you think I'm letting you paw through her postcards? You think I let every nut job pretending to be a *food* inspector into my room?"

Charlotte scowled.

Again, pointing out the food inspector slip.

"When did you know?" she asked, letting the jab slide.

"When I realized you lived in Estelle's house. After that, figuring out who you are was easy enough."

"How—Oh. I put my address on the card at check-in."

Angelina nodded and stood. "Right. It's not like I was rifling through your room." She flashed her toothy grin.

Charlotte turned to stare through the glass balcony doors.

I have a living grandfather. And an aunt!

She couldn't place the emotions roiling in her core. A little elation. A little fear? Where were these people when her mother died? Where were they when her *grandmother* died? They didn't come to get her. If it hadn't been for Mariska and Frank's pull with the authorities, she would have been sent to an *orphanage*. They didn't even come to the funeral—

Charlotte gasped.

In her mind's eye, she recalled her grandmother's funeral. It had almost been too much for her then, having so recently lost her mother to then lose her grandmother too, the last person on Earth related to her. Or so she thought. She remembered standing between Mariska and Darla, both hovering like protective mother birds.

She'd looked to the side to hide her welling tears from Mariska. She hadn't wanted her grandmother's well-meaning neighbor to see her pain and grab and hug her with that suffocating grip again. She wanted to be left alone.

That's when she saw him. The tall man stood beside a coconut palm on the outskirts of the cemetery, a thin trail of smoke rising from the cigarette between his fingers, clear against the dark wall of clusia bushes growing behind him.

She didn't know who he was then, and he was quickly forgotten when *Darla*, instead of Mariska, spotted her tears and stooped down to bear-hug her.

Was that my real grandfather lurking on the outskirts of the cemetery?

"I need to see him," she said.

"Who?"

"Shea. Mick. My *grandfather*. I have to see him."

Angelina nodded.

Charlotte forced her attention to the postcards again and pretended to look through them, but her thoughts consumed her attention. She'd gone from no family to twice as much family in a day.

What if she could find Siofra? What would she call her? Aunt Siofra? What about Shea McQueen? Should she call him Grandpa? Pop-Pop? Mick?

"Are you done with those?" asked Angelina.

Charlotte jerked from her daydreaming.

"What? No."

"You're done." Angelina leaned forward and tried to grab the wad of postcards.

Charlotte held them out of reach. "I'm not. I want to think about them."

"Think later." Angelina leaned back and sighed. "I'll let you keep them for a bit."

"Okay. Thank you. Can I see my grandfather now?"

Angelina smiled, a strange mischievous twinkle in her eye. "First, show me what you have in the shoebox."

CHAPTER FIFTEEN

Charlotte and Angelina took the elevator to room four eleven, and Charlotte swiped open the door. Inside, she moved to the safe and plugged in her dog's name as represented by the number each letter fell in the alphabet. It wasn't the greatest password, but it would have to have been a thorough thief to come up with it. Certainly, someone with a larger plan than the quick ransacking of a hotel room.

She slid out the shoebox and carried it to the small table to the right of the balcony doors. Angelina sat in one of the matching chairs, and Charlotte popped off the lid before moving to the room's mini-fridge. The salty soy sauce from her sushi lunch had her craving water.

"You can have a look. Can I get you something to drink?" she asked, retrieving a bottle of water.

Angelina held up a hand. "No, thank you. I'm working."

"I meant water."

Angelina's lip curled. "No, thank you."

Charlotte was about to head back to the table when she noticed an empty spot in the row of tiny airplane bottles lining the inside of the refrigerator door. She paused to count them; two rums, two scotches, *one* vodka.

I didn't notice that missing before.

She looked at Angelina. "There's a vodka missing."

"What's that?"

"There's a vodka missing from my fridge. I didn't drink it."

Angelina glanced up. "I'll tell the front desk not to charge you for it."

Charlotte stared at her as the woman returned to shuffling through the papers.

Hm.

She couldn't be certain, but she was starting to think Angelina could lie as easily as she breathed.

Charlotte moved through her room, inspecting things for signs of tampering. Nothing seemed out of place other than the vodka. She peeked into the safe again.

Has the shoebox been moved?

Her duffle bag sat in the same spot as where she'd left it. She hadn't thought to really look at it before pulling it out.

But is it tilted a little more to the right?

With a grunt and a silent vow to pay more attention from then on, she took a seat across from Angelina, who continued to paw through the box.

"See anything?" Charlotte asked.

"It's all long ago and far away." Angelina held up a child's drawing of a stick figure with short hair and round black circles for eyes. It looked as though the figure was holding a gun. "She was an adorable kid."

"He looks like a soldier. Is her father military?"

"Navy."

"So Mick raised her?"

Angelina snorted a laugh. "That might not be how Siofra described it. But yes."

"But that's why there are report cards from so many different schools? He moved her around?"

"They traveled a lot. It's a long story."

"I'd like to hear it."

"Maybe sometime." Angelina stood. "I have to get back to work. You can keep the postcards for as long as you need, but they don't leave the hotel. Deal?"

"Deal. But you have to take me to see my grandfather."

Angelina nodded as she moved toward the door. "I will. Of course. I'll, uh, talk to his nurse and arrange a time for tomorrow, okay?"

With no other option offered, Charlotte agreed.

With a tight smile, Angelina left.

CHAPTER SIXTEEN

At a quarter to six in the morning, a line of cars and trucks pulled into T.K.'s driveway, led by Ban and his father Foliage, who arrived in Targetville's only rainbow-painted Volkswagen Bug. Foliage hit the horn, playing an abbreviated version of *Give Peace a Chance*.

When all the vehicles had parked, nineteen cars filled the driveway, spilling over into the empty plot beside the tomato field.

"I've brought the protesters!" announced Foliage, unfolding himself from the Bug.

It was the first time Frank didn't mind seeing a bunch of hippies show up to a party.

He spotted Bob walking toward him with Declan at his side.

"Where's Charlotte?" he asked when they were close enough.

Declan shrugged. "She had to run to the East Coast."

Frank chuckled. "Bet you're happy it cleared up your day for this."

"Oh sure. Wouldn't miss it for the world." He looked at his watch. "We were going to show up at seven, but Bob couldn't sleep and asked me to come get him at five."

Frank laughed and glanced at Foliage, who'd started rallying his people with a bullhorn.

Declan followed his stare. "Let me guess—his father's the guy with the rainbow Bug?" asked.

Frank nodded. "Yep. Last time I saw him this happy, he was lobbying against the mind-altering rays of the Target's anti-theft beeper system."

Elizabeth, the Tomato Queen, walked through her front door to be greeted by a gaggle of women with various-sized picnic baskets.

"What's going on?" she called to Frank.

"Men are coming to tear up T.K.'s field. We're not going to let them."

Elizabeth gaped, but she didn't ask any more questions. Frank assumed she knew something about her field's impending doom-by-corporation, but knowing T.K., he guessed he hadn't wanted to worry his wife with details.

Foliage's ready-made protest group had grown to include hippies and homesteaders. Men with shotguns milled about T.K.'s yard, talking to each other as if it were just another day defending their compound from tax collectors. It struck Frank as an odd combination, but he imagined they both loved protesting in their way.

Frank caught Mac's eye and motioned him over.

"Hey, do me a favor. Try and keep the guys with guns away from the guys with the hemp shirts."

Mac's forehead furrowed. "Huh?"

"Keep the hippies away from the militia guys."

"Aw, they're all here to help Elizabeth."

Mac offered him a goofy grin, and Frank could tell he'd helped himself to a few more breakfast beers. He tried to speak a little slower.

"They're all on the same page now, but there are a few hot-button topics I don't want them sharing deep thoughts. They could go from protesting for T.K.'s farm to protesting against each other in a heartbeat."

Mac mulled this for a moment. "Yeah, I see what you're

saying."

"Good. Get Tommy to help you. Be casual."

Mac eased out a flat hand as if slipping it between two mattresses. "Casual. Cool. Totally cool. I can do that."

Frank frowned. *Yep. He definitely had a few more beers.*

Mac toddled off, and Frank surveyed the crowd, half of which were bouncing homemade signs with slogans like *"Hell no, Tomatoes Won't Go!"*

Bob wandered over. "How was your evening?"

"Uncomfortable and wet." Frank nodded at the crowd. "How did this happen?"

"Ban told his dad what was happening, and Foliage did the rest. Clubsoda spent all night making the posters for the hippie group."

"And the militia boys?"

"Not sure. Someone caught wind we were protesting government interference, and they were in like Flynn."

"But we're not. We're protesting a corporation."

Bob shrugged. "Same thing to them."

Frank stroked his mustache with his index finger. "I wonder if this is going to get out of hand."

"Nothing to wonder about, Frank." Bob grinned. "There's *no* way this is going to end well."

CHAPTER SEVENTEEN

Charlotte spent the rest of the evening staring at Siofra's postcards. She called up a turkey sandwich for dinner that cost more than her entire sushi lunch and ate it in front of her laptop, typing search after search about the locations from which the postcards arrived.

Bonding with the shifty concierge didn't get you discounts on room service.

Her previous evening investigating the leak in her ceiling exacted a final toll on her eyelids around eight p.m. She crawled into bed intending to take a quick nap.

She awoke in the dark.

The deafening silence told her she'd slept longer than she'd intended. Gone were the occasional voices floating down the hall and the crunching of tires on stone in the parking lot. Crickets refused to sing. It almost felt like the sound was being taken *out* of her ears. She had to admit, she liked not hearing the tinkle of her

Pineapple Port neighbor's wind chime for once.

Twisting her wrist to wake up her watch, she stared at the glowing numbers signifying five o'clock in the morning.

Well, I certainly can't complain about the bed.

It had been the first evening in a long time when Abby hadn't pushed a paw into her nose, mouth, or stomach. No wonder she'd slept so soundly.

Charlotte sat up and turned on the bedside table lamp to illuminate the room and the pile of postcards still strewn across the covers beside her.

Everything she'd discovered about those mysterious missives spilled back into her head.

It wasn't much.

If there was a code, she hadn't cracked it. She'd put them in order of sending date and tried every combination to find a pattern. The first letter of every city from which they were sent. The first letter of every state. Letters turned to numbers. Zip codes turned to letters. She'd scoured every nuance of every picture. The photos seemed entirely random as if Siofra hadn't taken any care in picking the images. Some were of the local attractions, some promotional postcards from restaurants where she'd probably eaten, and some were random animal shots with cutesy phrases on them. She particularly liked the one featuring a spotted, blue-ribbon porker with *Happy as a Pig in Mud!* scrawled across the front in a font that appeared fashioned out of hay. Siofra must have picked that one up at a 4-H Fair.

Charlotte picked up another card and stared at a picture of a lake full of ducks.

Why postcards at all? There were a million ways to send messages to people. Why wasn't she emailing? Was she frightened someone would trace her IP address back to her? Were Angelina and her father so sophisticated? Or was it someone *else* she feared?

Charlotte shook her head and tried to approach the puzzle from a new angle. How about money? How did Siofra afford to eat at restaurants and visit these attractions? Was she independently wealthy? Did she search out employment in each town? And if she did, was it always the same sort of job? The food cards implied maybe she picked up waitressing jobs. Then again, maybe she was a tour guide.

Charlotte jotted down a reminder to ask

Angelina about Siofra's resources and then spent a few minutes solving the greater mystery of how the tiny coffee maker sitting on top of the bureau worked. When it finally bubbled to life, she grabbed her computer and set it on her lap in bed. She shuffled through the postcards to find where she'd left off and started, again, plugging in the cities from which the cards had come.

Like the evening before, she found the locations had little in common. Some were small towns, some were large cities, and none seemed to share much other than people, houses, and postcards for sale.

Charlotte huffed.

There has to be a thread that connects these places.

Clearly, Siofra didn't want to be found. Why did she send postcards at all? If her father was motivated to find her, wouldn't he go to where the cards were sent from?

That would be too easy.

Charlotte sat up a little straighter.

Right. That would be too easy.

Siofra *wouldn't* send the cards from somewhere she could be found. That left two options: she either sent them from somewhere she *wasn't*—maybe towns she drove through—or she sent them from somewhere she *had been*. Past tense.

If she chose cards from towns between one place and another, random towns she drove through on her way to her next destination, then there had to be a reason she picked the cards she had. There had to be a pattern based on the towns' names or zip codes or something other than the places themselves. But Charlotte felt she'd already exhausted every possibility regarding patterns. If Siofra was using a code, like spelling out words using the first letter of the towns where she bought the cards, then it was in an alien language she didn't speak.

Charlotte slipped from beneath her laptop and poured a tiny creamer into her tiny paper coffee cup.

Maybe Angelina was wrong about Mick not understanding the cards. If Mick and his daughter had a secret language through which they communicated, she'd never crack the code. Maybe the jumbles of letters she'd generated from the cards made sense if you had a key.

If Mick had a key, it was probably in his

room. Maybe Angelina could help her look for it. She groaned, thinking about having to ask her. Getting Angelina to share anything was a chore—getting her to ransack Mick's room would be like pushing a boulder, wearing tights and heels, up a hill.

Charlotte slipped back into bed and put the coffee on the nightstand and the computer on her lap.

The other option was that the towns were places she *had been in*. But again, they didn't seem to have anything in common—

Except the date she'd visited them. They all had a *time* when she'd been there. All different dates, of course, but why *then*?

Charlotte started typing cities and dates into her laptop.

She scrolled through the results for Decatur, Illinois, three years previously in April.

A few newspaper articles popped up, including one about a missing girl who'd been found alive and one about a local man who'd won a prize at a car show in Chicago.

Hm.

The car show prize didn't seem important, but the missing girl piqued her interest.

She tried Austin, Texas. A new library wing opening. *Yawn.* A woman sent to jail for killing her husband in an elaborate plot.

Double hm.

Laramie, Wyoming—another murderer captured.

Charlotte looked up.

This is it.

She hit back on the browser and tried to find more information about the missing girl found in Decatur. In an article, the police thanked the public for their help in finding the girl. In Austin, the authorities again thanked anonymous tips for pointing them in the right direction.

Charlotte plugged in a few more dates and cities from the postcards. A couple didn't seem to click, but most did.

Charlotte shook, a giddy thrill running through her body.

She's solving crimes anonymously.

My aunt is some kind of vigilante detective.

What were the chances they'd be in the same line of work?

Charlotte reached over to grab her cooling coffee and take a sip. She grimaced. It tasted sour. She was pretty sure coffee wasn't supposed to taste *sour*.

Didn't matter. The coffee wasn't going to sour her mood.

Ha!

She missed having Declan and Abby around to abuse with her puns.

Charlotte moved the laptop and swung her legs over the bed.

Maybe I should tell Angelina.

She looked at her watch. It was only six.

Too early. Grr.

But that's okay. She'd found the pattern. Now all they had to do was figure out what crime Siofra would solve next.

Her shoulders slumped.

How the heck are we going to do that?

CHAPTER EIGHTEEN

"Did you see this?"

Hunter glanced over at the police officer lying in her motel bed. He held aloft a newspaper, the one she'd bought for herself. She'd turned away for one second, and he'd grabbed it, and now she sat at the peeling, laminated table drinking coffee and staring out the window at the parking lot, mulling on her oh-so-glamorous life.

She looked at him. "No, I didn't see it because you stole my paper."

Hunter smiled to show she didn't mind and studied the line of Officer Kevin's manly nose and the curl of his lips to create a last mental picture of him. Kevin was a nice guy. She'd been lucky to work with him over the past few months. She'd miss him a little.

"Some chick swapped a baby," he said, still staring at the paper, unaware she was cataloging him.

Hunter laughed. "What?"

"Some chick's kid was taken, and the cops thought they got it back, but it turns out it was a different baby."

"That's crazy."

"Totally."

Hunter lifted her phone and tried to read the newsfeed but found her mind returning to the kidnapped baby.

"Where was this?" she asked.

"Hm?" Kevin had moved on to the sports page.

"The baby swap. Where did it happen? Here?"

He shook his head. "Oh, no. I forget."

She continued to stare at him until he glanced up and noticed. "You want me to check?"

"Yes, please."

He picked up another piece of paper and opened it to skim the page.

"Florida. Jupiter Beach, Florida."

Hunter heard herself release a tiny gasp. Her hands and face went tingly. It felt like someone had flipped a switch in her body and charged her veins with a low buzz of electricity.

It can't be.

She leaned forward, her hand outstretched.

"Give me that."

He handed her the paper, and she folded it to the page he'd been reading. She felt the ink on her fingers and thought, no wonder *many people read their news online*. Still, she liked the feel of holding a book when she read. Sometimes it was nice to have something *not* glowing in her eyeballs.

Kevin sniffed. "Hey, you know, I was thinking. I mean, now that we solved the case, maybe you don't need to live in a motel—"

"Nope. Not a good idea." She answered without hearing him, but she could tell by the sniff that he was about to say something he feared she wouldn't like. Add that to his softened tone, and she knew where the conversation was headed.

He peppered his soft tone with a hint of irritation. "Whaddya mean? You don't even know what I was going to say."

She lowered the paper.

"You were going to ask me if I wanted to move in. We'd spend a few months finding out we don't have anything in common except finding that little girl. We'll start fighting about how you put the toilet paper on the roll backward—"

"But I *don't* put it on backward—"

"—and how I leave my socks on the floor. Then I'll move out, and we will have wasted what good years we have left on a pipedream."

He stared at her, his eyebrows raised and hopes dashed. *Maybe.* She didn't think he was as invested in her as maybe he was fooling himself into believing. Kevin was a lovely, honest man, but they'd never had that *thing.* She suspected he knew that too, somewhere in that ruggedly handsome head of his.

He scratched at his graying stubble. "Jeeze. Tell me what you *really* think."

"That's one thing you'd never have to wonder about," she said, returning to the paper.

"You're getting old to be alone," he added after a measured pause.

She looked up. *Ouch.*

"Don't lash out. It's not sexy," she scolded.

He grunted, and she stood.

"Anyway, it's not you. It's me. I have to go."

"Go where?"

"Away. Leave Concord."

"You're *leaving* leaving?"

She nodded and stuffed the few things she hadn't packed while he was sleeping into the overnight bag that served as her world.

"Where?" he asked. The soft tone had returned.

She shrugged, thinking she didn't know, but she'd already slipped the paper with the story about the baby swap into her bag. She knew what that meant.

He tried again. "When were you going to tell me this?"

"I just did. Anyway, that girl at the coffee shop has been dying to go out with you."

"Who? Janice?" he scowled as if he was offended she thought he'd be interested in another woman, but the corners of his mouth couldn't help but curl up.

She chuckled. Kevin would be just fine without her.

"Yes, Janice."

"Why would you say that?"

She rolled her eyes. "Don't be stupid. You know."

"Yeah, but, I mean, she's not *you*—"

She leaned forward and tussled his hair. "Oh stop. I'm not *me*, either. You've only seen me at my best, both of us in the heat of a case. Day-to-day, I'm a pain in the neck."

He grinned and grabbed her wrist to pull her towards him. "I never doubted that."

She pecked him on the lips and cupped his jaw with her palm to stare into his eyes.

"You're a good guy, Kevin." She kissed her finger and pressed it into the middle of his forehead.

He took a deep breath and then blew it out through puffed cheeks as she pulled away. He let her hand slip through his.

"Man, you've got it all figured out."

She laughed. "Oh sure. That's me."

Hunter scooped up her bag and then paused with her hand on the doorknob. She returned to the nightstand and lifted Kevin's gun belt. Underneath it lay a postcard she'd bought on her first day in town featuring a picture of maple trees being tapped. It was already filled out with a mailing address and a stamp she'd stolen from Kevin's desk drawer at the police station.

Kevin watched her.

"I thought for a second there you'd changed your mind."

She shook her head. "Tell Janice I said goodbye. Tell her she was the best damn barista I've ever known."

He snorted a laugh. "Yeah, yeah."

Bag in one hand and postcard in the other, Hunter left. She walked to the motel office and dropped the postcard in the outgoing mail before hopping in her car and pointing south.

CHAPTER NINETEEN

Seven a.m. came and went as Frank watched restless protesters rise, wave, and crouch through mock march-ins and sit-downs. By eight, a full party had broken out. Children played tag, Clubsoda touched up his posters, militia men marched, and Foliage demonstrated how to squat so you couldn't be moved.

At first, no one noticed the single bulldozer, silhouetted by the morning sun, rising into view like a mechanical dinosaur. It crept closer to the field, belching smoke until a child running too far from the group spotted the cigar-chomping driver and a suited man hanging from the cabin. She ran back to alert the group, screaming as if she'd spotted a killer clown.

Frank stretched his back, heard his spine crack with the effort, and made a mental note to never, never, *ever* sleep anywhere but in his bed again. He watched the child running toward the group, waving her hands above her head and screaming words he couldn't make out.

"Here we go."

A bulldozer chugged over the horizon and stopped short of the bomb fence surrounding the tomato field. A suited man raised his bullhorn, one newer and shinier than Foliage's.

"You, people! Disperse! This is private land!"

Frisbee and paddleball games ceased as the party's attention swiveled to the mechanical yellow monster lurking at the far edge of the field.

"Raise your posters!" screamed Foliage.

The crowd scrambled for their protesting accouterments. Someone started singing 'My Country 'tis of Thee.'

Mac, Frank, Bob, Tommy, and Declan made their way to the far bomb fence, Tommy filming the entire scene from behind his iPhone.

"This is all a little dramatic for one of your films, isn't it?" Bob asked him. "And doesn't everyone have to be naked?"

Tommy shrugged. "I'm growing as an artist."

Declan scowled. "Did you say *naked*?"

Mac cleared his throat and called out over the steady rumble of the bulldozer. "You move another inch, and you'll go up in a cloud of fine powder, buddy!"

Frank recognized the suited man as the one who'd visited them in the bar the night before. He cupped his hands around his mouth to make himself a homemade bullhorn.

"I've put in a call to a judge. You're going to have to cease and desist," he yelled over the din of the machine.

"You have papers?" asked the suited man through his much louder bullhorn.

Frank frowned and dropped his hands from his mouth.

Showoff.

Tommy lowered his camera and motioned at the bulldozer. "Can you turn off that thing? It's messing with the dialogue."

The man said something to his driver, and the bulldozer's engine cut. He dropped off the cabin and walked toward the men, pointing at Tommy.

"Your chin is still red," he said.

Tommy raised his phone to cover his chin.

Frank cleared his throat. "Look. The injunction will be here before you can climb back into that thing—"

Foliage appeared at Frank's elbow with his own ancient bullhorn pointed at the suited man.

"Hell no, we won't go! Hell no, we won't go—"

Wincing, Frank snatched the bullhorn from him.

"Are you out of your mind?"

He pushed it against Foliage's chest and readdressed the suited man.

"Look, mister, this is the Tomato King's land. He hasn't even been dead a month. His widow is still in shock. Let's work something out."

Behind him, 'Give Peace a Chance' surged from the crowd camped in T.K.'s back yard.

The suited man strolled to one of the dummy bombs lining the field. He ran his hand over their yellow-grey surface and rapped them with his knuckle. He looked at Frank with a smug smile.

"I'm afraid you don't know who you're dealing with here, gentlemen." He stepped back and upgraded his smug smirk to an evil grin. "My name's Andrew Hepper, and my father was a *Major* on this base. I know dummy bombs when I see one."

The jaws of all four Gophers fell slack.

"Little Andy?" said Mac, holding a hip-high hand to show Andrew Hepper's height the last time he'd seen him.

"A little jerk, just like your father," grumbled Bob.

Andrew Hepper straightened. "My father was a great man."

The Gophers burst into laughter.

"I've seen your dad naked more times than my mailman," said Tommy.

Declan's gaze snapped to Frank. "He sees his *mailman* naked?"

Frank waved away his question. "Long story. Later."

Andrew looked as confused as Declan. "What are you talking about?"

Mac waved his open palms like slow-motion jazz hands. "Your father and his secretary taught me *everything* I know about sex. Which, I have to tell you, has caused me more than a little trouble with the ladies over the years. Turns out pretending to have shrapnel in your thigh isn't the *norm*."

Andrew's cheeks flashed crimson. "You're lying."

"No. It's true. They didn't teach sex education back then," said Bob.

The other Gophers shook their heads. "Nope."

Declan ran a hand through his hair. "I have *so* many questions."

Andrew Hepper appeared as though something had lodged in his throat. He covered his ears with his hands, his mouth lipping what looked to Frank like, "No, no, no, no..." over and over.

Declan leaned toward Mac. "I think you might have hit a raw nerve there."

Frank overheard and grunted. It looked like Mac wasn't the only person Major Hepper's sexual predilections had sent to therapy.

Andrew lowered his hands from his ears and swallowed. He smoothed his tie against his chest and lifted his chin to cast a beady gaze toward Tommy.

"Who *are* you?"

"We're the kids whose names your father painted on bomb targets to scare us away from these dummy bombs," said Tommy. He cupped his hands and pointed toward the crowd behind them. "This guy's Major Hepper's son!"

Tommy's announcement had no effect.

"They're too young to remember Major Hepper," muttered Frank.

Tommy sighed, shoulders slumping. "When did we get so old?"

Foliage turned back to the crowd, his expression twisting with what looked like horror. "What are they *singing*?"

Frank realized the crowd was in the middle of a round of 'Row, Row, Row Your Boat.'

Before he could return to his conversation with Andrew, Hepper's son huffed, lifted his hands in the air, and dropped them to his sides with a slap. "Why am I even talking to you people?" He turned on his heel and marched back to the bulldozer to climb to his spot hanging from the driver's cage. "This place is as good as gone. You've got no papers and no right to stop us."

He tapped the driver's shoulder, and the tractor roared again.

"Are you sure those bombs ain't real?" Frank heard the driver scream over the tractor's rumble.

"Fake!" answered Andrew, thrusting his hand into the air like a fascist dictator punctuating a speech.

The Gophers, Declan, and Foliage fell back a few steps as the bulldozer lurched forward.

"Now what?" asked Tommy.

One of the children ran up and threw a tomato at the tractor. It struck the top of the front grill, splattering the driver with a mist of red slime and seeds.

"Take that!" the child arced around and slipped between two bombs, presumably to find another missile in the field.

Frank and the others watched the child go, gazes settling on the plants beyond the bombs, each bursting with red and green fruit.

"You thinking what I'm thinking?" asked Mac.

Frank checked his watch. "Well, we *do* need to kill about fifteen minutes before that injunction gets here."

Mac grinned and led the charge into the field. His first tomato hit the bulldozer driver square on the forehead, covering him with tomato blood.

"I'm not doing this," screamed the driver as he cut the engine.

"What?" shrieked Andrew, his voice too loud as the engine shuddered to a halt.

"I don't like it and don't need it." The driver slid from his seat to the opposite side of the tractor to avoid flying produce and jogged away.

Holding up his arm to block flying tomatoes, Andrew took the driver's seat and restarted the tractor. He shifted some levers, and the bulldozer jerked forward, its shovel knocking over three dummy bombs. Two more fell like dominos.

Declan picked up a child and scooted him out of harm's way.

From his location in the field, Frank spotted a small group of militiamen advancing from the collection of protesters. They lined up like British soldiers, shotguns aimed at the bulldozer.

Frank frowned.

Crap.

"You can't shoot me, you idiots!" Hepper shrieked. "You can't murder people over gardens, in front of witnesses!"

More yellow-grey bombs tumbled passively to the ground as Andrew's lemon-hued mount leapt forward again.

"My father knew you were watching him with his secretary! I watched him too!"

"Ooh, boy. There it is. Thirty years of therapy gone in a heartbeat." said Bob. "He's crazy as a jaybird."

The protest party's voices swelled.

"Eighty bottles of beer on the wall, eighty bottles of beer."

Foliage spun and threw a tomato in the direction of the crowd. "That's not what I told you to sing!" He stomped back toward the yard, waving his hands above his head. "Stop! Stop!"

Andrew and the tractor continued up the row of bombs, knocking them flat and rolling over a few, maniacally laughing as tomatoes exploded around him.

"He's going to tear up the place before we can stop him," said Frank.

Declan looked up, shielding his eyes from the sun with his palm. "What's that?"

A second engine's roar buzzed above them. Frank squinted skyward and spotted a crop-dusting plane, its blue wings tilting back and forth like a levitating see-saw.

Fierce goblin tomato faces, painted on the wings after The Great Tomato War, caught the sunlight in their angry eyes and flashed furious warnings at the bulldozer.

Mac turned his attention to the sky and then looked at Frank, his eyes wide.

"It's T.K.!"

CHAPTER TWENTY

Charlotte took the elevator to the lobby to find Angelina. The concierge desk sat unoccupied. Croix was at her station with her back turned, so Charlotte headed down the hallway to Angelina's door. She knocked, but no one answered.

Shoot.

She'd hoped to go over her findings.

Turning back to the lobby, she nearly plowed into Croix, who'd somehow walked down the hall without Charlotte hearing her and now stood beside her. The experience felt like a haunted house statue that followed people when they weren't looking.

Charlotte stepped back to catch her balance and focus on the creeper.

"Where'd you come from?" she asked without thinking of a cooler response. Her nervous giggle didn't help her *cool* factor one iota.

"Pennsylvania," said Croix without smiling. "Looking for Angelina?"

Charlotte cleared her throat. "Yes. I have some information for her."

"She's not in yet."

"She doesn't live here?"

Croix turned and headed back down the hall. "She'll be in soon."

Charlotte watched her go.

That wasn't what I asked.

Charlotte looked at the door again and thought she saw a shadow pass by the peephole on the inside.

"Fine," she said as if calling out to Croix. "I'll tell her I figured out where Siofra is when she returns."

If Angelina lurked behind the door, she must have heard her.

She wandered back down the hall and into the continental breakfast room to see if the coffee there tasted any better than the stuff made by her miniature coffee pot back in the room. It was, so she took a cup and a Danish to the lobby and found a seat by the concierge desk. Fifteen minutes later, Angelina appeared at the end of the hall leading to her bedroom with Harley tucked under her arm.

"I knew you were in there," said Charlotte.

Angelina blinked at her, bleary-eyed. "It's a little early for me."

Harley squiggled, her eyes locked on Charlotte, begging for attention. Charlotte scratched her beneath her ear. "But you wanted to know what I figured out about Siofra?"

Angelina shook her head. "Not until I've had some coffee." She shuffled into the breakfast room and reappeared to sit behind the concierge desk.

"Okay. Hit me," she said.

Charlotte crossed her arms against her chest. "Not until you take me to see my grandfather."

Ha ha! Who has the power now?

She tried not to look smug.

Angelina tilted back her head and let her mouth hang open. "Come *on*. I got up early to hear this."

"So take me to see him, and then I'll tell you."

"It's barely eight o'clock."

"So? You said he's in a coma. What does he care what time it is?"

"Excellent point." Angelina lowered her chin again. "He would have appreciated the dark humor of that."

She stood and walked to the elevator. Charlotte jumped to her feet to follow.

Angelina pulled a key from a chain from the nest of her bosom and used it to unlock the top-floor elevator button. When the lift's doors opened again, Charlotte faced a hallway with only three doors along the opposite wall. Angelina knocked on the one directly across from the elevator and let herself in with a code. The door featured the same keypad as Angelina's room.

The apartment inside was expansive. Someone had bashed away the walls of the individual hotel rooms to create one giant open-plan suite featuring a large living room and kitchen to the right of the entrance. Style-wise, nothing appeared modern or updated beyond the open plan itself, but neither was it hopelessly outdated. Furniture, walls, and floors were all variations of brown, black, and white—the overall vibe felt too dark for Florida, but it didn't seem unusual for a bachelor's apartment. Charlotte guessed her grandfather didn't have a current wife. A woman would have included a splash of color or warmth *somewhere*.

A woman much too young to be Mick's wife and dressed in nurse's scrubs sat on a black leather sofa. Her loose-fitting clothes were covered in tiny teddy bears wearing Santa hats, making her easily the most festive thing in the room. She looked up from her book as they entered.

"I've brought a visitor," said Angelina. "You can stay. Martisha, this is Charlotte. You might see her again. She's one of us."

The woman smiled in Charlotte's direction. "Ow yuh do?" she asked in a thick Jamaican accent.

Charlotte smiled back. "Nice to meet you."

The woman nodded and returned to her reading.

Angelina led Charlotte through a partially opened door into a bedroom decorated in much the same style, but whatever bed might have once sat between the two dark wooden bedside tables had been replaced by a hospital bed with chrome side rails and an adjustable base. A thin, wiry man lay in the bed looking both tan and ashen at the same time. His salt-and-pepper hair had been cropped short. Charlotte could tell he'd been handsome and still was, she supposed, for a seventy-plus-year-old man in a coma. Taped to his arms were tubes of various thicknesses and colors.

"There he is," said Angelina, her usual steady expression softened by what looked to Charlotte to be genuine sadness. She motioned to Mick, urging Charlotte to get as close as she needed.

Charlotte moved to the edge of the bed and rested her fingers on the bed rails to peer down at Mick, unsure what to do now that she'd confirmed he existed.

"He's not much of a conversationalist lately," said Angelina, breaking the ice.

"Can he hear anything?"

"I don't know. They say he probably can. I'll talk to him anyway."

Charlotte swallowed and turned her attention back to Mick.

What should I say?

"Hi, I'm not sure what to call you," she said, her voice sounding weak. She wasn't sure why she felt so moved by the quiet dignity of the man lying in the bed before her. She didn't know him. Maybe he wasn't even really related to her. But it was heartbreaking to see someone laid so low even if he was a total stranger.

Angelina broke the following silence.

"He'd hate *grandpa*, I can tell you that," she muttered.

"I wasn't going to call him *grandpa*."

"I'm just saying."

Charlotte took a cleansing breath and tried again. "I'm your granddaughter, apparently. My mother was Grace. I don't know if you knew her or if she knew you at all. I'm not even entirely sure if you were her father. I'm going by what Angelina told me."

Angelina sniffed. "You can't talk about me like I'm not in the room."

"Well, it's true. I could be telling him all this, and he could think, *who is this crazy girl?* I don't *know* if he was my mother's father."

"He was."

"How do you know?"

"He told me."

Charlotte grimaced. "Doesn't mean it's true."

Angelina cocked an eyebrow. "Do you want me to ask Martisha to tap a vein so you can run some tests? Maybe you'd like to pluck a hair off his head?"

Charlotte lowered her eyes, feeling guilty she'd already thought about stealing a hair.

Though maybe hair wasn't the way to go.

She'd taken a DNA test before, and all the online service needed was some *spit*. If Angelina left the room, it might be easy enough to grab some drool without getting needles involved...

Charlotte shook her head.

I'm turning into a ghoul.

"Your mother is the reason he took Siofra."

Lost in her thoughts, it took Charlotte a moment to digest Angelina's statement. "What?"

Angelina sighed. "That was the deal he made with Estelle. She kept the first kid, so he got the second."

Charlotte felt her eyes bug. "What sort of thing is that? Who has *occasional* children with someone and then doles them out like playing cards?" She pantomimed dealing. "One for me, one for you..."

Angelina smirked. "Estelle and Mick, apparently. I don't think either of the kids were exactly *planned*."

Charlotte lifted her hands and let them slap back to her thighs. "Oh, for crying out loud. Now I'm the byproduct of an *oops*."

"Maybe *you* were an oops, too," suggested Angelina, studying her nails.

Charlotte gaped. "What? Did you know my mother, too?"

"No. I'm just saying. It's possible. I might have been an oops too. Maybe we're all oopses."

"Are you crazy? Is everyone in this hotel crazy?"

Angelina shrugged without looking up. "Open for interpretation."

Charlotte turned back to Mick and tried to block Angelina's presence out of her mind. "Anyway, Mick, I'm your granddaughter, according to the crazy lady behind me. And I think I might have found your other daughter, Siofra."

Charlotte thought she saw a flick of movement near Mick's mouth and leaned forward to watch. Nothing else happened.

"Are you going to kiss him?" asked Angelina.

Charlotte straightened. "*No*, I think he moved."

"What?"

"His lip twitched when I mentioned Siofra."

"He does that. Used to freak me out, but Martisha told me it doesn't mean anything. Tell him what you figured out about Siofra."

Charlotte rolled her eyes. "You're trying to trick me into telling *you* what I figured out." She paused. "I was going to tell you anyway."

"I know. I don't think I'm tricking you."

"You do, a little."

Angelina bobbed her head from side to side. "Maybe a little."

"I'm telling you. You're not tricking me."

"Okay."

Charlotte took a deep breath. "The postcards are from cities with sensational crimes."

Angelina scowled. "What does that mean?"

"It means she reads about crimes, online, I assume, or sees

them on television maybe, and then she goes to wherever they've taken place to solve them."

Angelina's expression didn't change.

"You don't think that's interesting?" Charlotte felt her annoyance shift to a new level.

"Sounds like Siofra. I'm more disappointed I didn't think of it."

"Yeah, well. I'm pretty sure that's what she's doing. I looked up the cities where the postcards came from, and they were almost always sent the day someone cracked the case. If it was a missing child, the child was found on the day the postcard was postmarked. Etcetera, etcetera."

"Why *almost*?"

"I couldn't connect a couple of the locations to crimes, but I think that's just a lack of news about that particular event. Those postcards need more Googling."

Angelina tapped her front teeth with her index finger. "So we have to figure out what crime she's going to solve next and then run to that town?"

Charlotte frowned. "That's the tough part. Thanks to the twenty-four-hour news cycle, a sensational new crime is reported every five minutes."

Angelina mumbled something.

"What?"

"I said I got another postcard from her yesterday."

"One you didn't give me?"

"Right. Brand new. From Concord, New Hampshire."

Charlotte straightened. "What day was it postmarked?"

"I don't know. We can go back to my room and check it."

Charlotte glanced back at Mick. She wanted to get to know him as much as she could in his condition, but she also wanted to go look at that postmark and start trying to find Siofra's new case. It seemed a shame to leave Mick so soon. He was her only family, other than Siofra. It figured she'd finally find family members, only to have one in a coma and another lost on the road.

She touched his hand, sliding her fingers down his own until her hand covered his. His thumb branched to the right and hers to the left, creating a double-thumbed hand.

Grandpa. Pop pop? Gramps?

"Can I come visit again?" she asked.

Angelina stood. "Are you asking me or him?"

"Both, though I think you're going to have to do the heavy lifting on the answer."

"Sure. Whenever. But for now, let's go find Siofra."

From the corner of her eye, Charlotte thought she saw another movement on Mick's face.

"Is it possible he's smiling a little?" she asked.

Angelina moved to the bed and peered down at him.

"Sometimes I think that, too."

Angelina leaned down to kiss him on the forehead, rubbed her lipstick off his skin with her thumb, and left the room.

Charlotte leaned down and whispered in Mick's ear.

"I'm going to bring Siofra back to you."

She watched for a reaction and, seeing none, scurried after Angelina. As she jogged by, she offered Martisha a wave, and the tiny woman waved back.

"Is the postcard in your room?" Charlotte asked as they slipped out the front door.

"My desk."

In the elevator, Charlotte nodded and took a deep breath, trying to sort through her feelings. As the elevator bounced to a halt, she decided now wasn't the time to process. Too many distractions. She tucked away her reaction to meeting Mick for later.

She realized Angelina hadn't said a word the entire way down, which was strange for her chatty new friend. Maybe Angelina had some feelings she needed to tuck away as well. She'd tried to play *tough girl* up in the room, but Charlotte could tell she had feelings for Mick. More than likely, they'd been seeing each other when he had his accident.

What happened to him?

"Hey, you never said what happened—"

The doors opened, and Angelina strode to her desk, leaving Charlotte and her question behind.

Charlotte shut her mouth and followed.

Okay. I'll ask that one later.

Angelina pulled open the single center drawer of her desk and retrieved a postcard with a maple syrup harvest scene on the front.

Charlotte took it, studied the image, and then flipped it over. The Concord, New Hampshire, postmark covered the stamp in the upper right corner.

"I thought *Vermont* was the maple syrup place," she said, as much to herself as Angelina.

Angelina sat in her chair. "Maybe that's a hint. Maybe Vermont is where she's going next."

Charlotte only found what she expected—the address of the Loggerhead Inn written in neat print in black ink, a stamp, a postmark, and nothing else. Most of the letters were capitals, except the g's in Loggerhead, whose tails hung down.

"I need to look up what happened in Concord recently."

Angelina swept a *voila!* motion in the direction of her opened laptop and stood.

"Search away."

With a glance at Croix, who, as usual, watched from her post at the front desk, Charlotte sat down and typed 'Concord, New Hampshire news crime' into the search engine.

Nothing popped up, so she tried 'Concord, New Hampshire, kidnapping.'

Nothing again.

She tried. 'Concord, New Hampshire newspaper' to find The Monitor. On the Monitor's website, she found it difficult to find things from a previous date but lucked out and spotted a follow-up story about a recently solved murder in the current day's copy.

"Here it is. This has to be it," she said, reading the article.

"How can you tell?"

"It's about a woman and her dog who went missing. They found them both alive."

"Siofra had a thing for animals," said Angelina.

"That might have had something to do with it, but it was an unsolved case. The dog returned home with the missing woman's wedding ring tied to her collar, two years after they both went missing."

Angelina's eyes widened. "Ooh, that *is* interesting."

"That's what I'm thinking. I could see how that might have captured her attention."

"Tell me more. They found her? Siofra found the woman?"

"It doesn't say anything about her, specifically, but it never does. Everything I found always credited an anonymous tip or someone else. This time it sounds like a local cop found her."

"Where?" asked Croix from across the room. Apparently, besides seeing all, she had the ears of an owl.

"In the neighbor's basement. He'd kidnapped her and the dog, and she finally found a way to get the dog out of the house."

"Yikes," said Croix.

"Why kidnap the dog?" asked Angelina.

Charlotte looked at her. "Maybe to use against the woman and keep her quiet?" it was a fair question but an odd detail to focus on first.

Angelina tucked Harley closer to her chest and kissed her on the top of her head. "Monster. I'd never let anyone kidnap you."

Harley remained nonplussed. No doubt she took for granted *nothing* would ever happen to her.

"Does it say anything about *any* other woman?" asked Angelina.

"Like who?"

"Siofra could be using another name. She used to do that a

lot working with her father."

Charlotte twisted in her chair to look at Angelina. "When were you going to tell me that?"

She shrugged. "I figured you knew."

"How would I know?"

"Because if she were using her real name, we would have found her ourselves long ago."

Charlotte sighed. She opened a new tab, closed her eyes, and let her fingers hover over the keys.

Angelina poked her in the back. "I'm pretty sure you have to type something for a search engine to work."

Charlotte scowled. "I'm thinking."

"About what?"

"I'm trying to think like her."

Angelina snorted a laugh. "Oh, okay."

Charlotte turned. "There are a million crimes out there. I want to try and narrow the field a little."

Angelina flashed both palms, Harley tucked in the crook of her armpit. "I stand corrected. By all means, please don't let me break your concentration."

Charlotte faced the laptop and closed her eyes again.

Think. Think. What are you looking for? Where do you want to go?

Behind her, Angelina made a ghostly noise. "Chaaaarlotte...this is Siofra... why are you caaaaalling meeee..."

Charlotte swiveled in her chair again. "I'm not trying to *summon her from the dead.*"

"I would hope not," muttered Croix from her lookout.

Angelina took Harley in both hands and bobbed her up and down in front of Charlotte's face as if she were a ghost, tiny legs dangling. She booped the dog's wet nose against hers until Charlotte had to wipe the moisture from her face. She tucked back her chin, trying not to laugh.

"You're making this a lot harder than it has to be," she said.

Angelina pulled Harley back against her arm, laughing.

"I'm sorry. Go ahead. What are you doing now?"

Charlotte huffed. Angelina hadn't taken a breath between giving her a moment and asking a new question. "I'm trying to find a pattern. For instance, those postcards moved from here, out west, floated around there for years, and then headed back this way. The last one was in New Hampshire, so I think I want to limit my searches to the east coast. She doesn't seem to hop from one end of the country to the other and back again."

Angelina nodded. "Okay. That makes sense. Proceed."

"Thanks."

"Driving distance?"

"That's what I'm thinking. And an overwhelming number of the cases were about missing children, too."

Angelina poked her again. "Type in 'missing children near Concord.'"

"I don't think that's how she does it. I think she tries to find *big* cases. National news cases and then picks one nearby she thinks sounds interesting."

"That's how I'd do it," mumbled Croix.

"What do you mean that's how you'd do it?" asked Angelina.

Croix shrugged. "If I could work on any case I wanted, I'd search for fun or challenging ones. Ones I thought other people couldn't solve."

Angelina shoved Charlotte's shoulder with her fingertips. "Do that."

Charlotte glared at her. "Quit poking me."

Angelina's eyes grew wide as she peered down her nose at Charlotte. "Sorry, Miss Sensitive."

Charlotte grit her teeth and returned her attention to the keyboard.

Think. Think.

She searched for the latest cases capturing the nation's attention.

"Oh my," she said after a few searches.

"What?"

"Look at this."

Charlotte pushed back her chair to make room for Angelina to lean in. The concierge manifested her reading glasses from somewhere in her cleavage.

"Do you have lunch in there, too?" asked Charlotte.

Angelina ignored her and popped on her glasses. She read the screen, her glossy crimson lips moving in time with the words. After a moment, she gasped.

"That's her."

"What? What is it?" asked Croix.

"Some woman had her baby kidnapped and then returned, but the baby returned wasn't *hers*."

"Someone swapped babies on her?" The bridge of Croix's nose wrinkled. "I don't have a kid, but why would anyone do that? Who wouldn't prefer their *own* baby?"

Angelina and Croix both trained their attention on Charlotte. Even Harley stared down at her with her big brown eyes.

Charlotte put her hand on her chest. "Why are you asking me?"

"You're the detective," said Angelina.

Charlotte sighed. "I don't know. Maybe they didn't like the baby they had."

Angelina scoffed. "Everyone likes their own baby best."

Croix nodded. "That is *weird*."

"Well, I don't know *why* they did it, but the swapped baby makes for an interesting case," said Charlotte.

Angelina straightened. "I don't know. The more I think about it, it might not be interesting enough. I mean, the last one with the dog—"

"Did you see where it is?" interrupted Charlotte.

"No. Where?"

Charlotte pointed to the top of the article, pressing her finger right under the words *Jupiter Beach*.

Angelina pointed to the ground. "It's *here*?"

Charlotte started typing. She asked Google Maps how long it would take to drive from Concord, New Hampshire, to Jupiter Beach, Florida. Google spat out the results.

"It's a full day's drive. Twenty-three hours. She'd probably at least split it."

"The postcard arrived yesterday, but it was mailed three days ago," said Angelina.

"So she *could* be here right now."

Angelina pressed her lips tightly and began to pace. "Do you think? Would she come here after all this time?"

"She might. She's been getting closer. Could be she was trying to make her way here anyway."

"Maybe *she's* the one who stole the baby, so she could come *here* and solve the case," offered Croix.

Angelina and Charlotte looked at her.

"Don't be an idiot," said Angelina.

Croix shrugged.

Charlotte glanced through the front entryway. "The question is, if she *is* here, where would she be?"

"Not here, apparently," mumbled Angelina.

"Getting involved with the case?" suggested Croix.

"Exactly." Charlotte looked at Angelina. "I need to borrow Harley."

CHAPTER TWENTY-ONE

Frank spotted the goblins on the crop duster and suffered a flashback to times gone by.

"It's T.K.!" repeated Mac, pointing at the plane.

Frank nodded. It was the same plane the Gophers had watched turn back the Air Force from Herbert's land so many years ago.

"But it can't be T.K.," he mumbled, squinting into the sun.

In Elizabeth Weeble's back yard, a hundred arms pointed toward the sky.

Hepper shifted the bulldozer into another gear and continued his path of destruction, unpeppered by tomatoes as his enemies' attentions drew skyward. Soon, he was far enough down the line of bombs even Declan's tossed tomatoes couldn't reach him anymore. The yellow monster approached the far corner of the fence, marked by a silver dummy bomb, chugging away as bombs pressed into the dirt beneath its giant tires.

The plane passed overhead and made an arcing loop to head back toward the field. As it approached, it swooped low, and even Hepper had to stop his progress to stare. Just as Frank feared the plane might plow directly into the bulldozer, the nose of the aircraft lifted toward the heavens, and the payload doors opened. Hundreds of red orbs cascaded over Hepper, the bulldozer, and the field exploding with gushy ferocity.

One red ball smacked Frank in the chest, and he took a step back to catch his balance. He looked down to find his uniform covered with red and suffered a moment of panic. He spotted seeds and realized he wasn't dying.

"Tomatoes?" he asked as the deflated skin of one slid down his buttons and slapped to the ground.

The bulldozer, now painted red with tomato blood, continued to grind toward the corner of the field.

That's when it exploded.

Declan and the Gophers dove to their bellies, crushing tomato plants beneath them, hands covering their heads. Dirt rained.

The crowd, already silenced by the plane, released a collective gasp.

When the soil stopped falling, Frank saw the plane veer hard to the right. It half-landed, half-crashed into the empty field behind the tomato farm.

A cloud of smoke rose from where the bulldozer had been and wafted toward the Gophers.

"What the hell was that?' asked Mac.

Frank dragged himself up, coughing, and lowered a hand to help pull Mac to his feet.

"What happened?" asked Declan as he helped Bob to his feet.

"T.K. came back from the dead to save his farm," said Mac.

Certain his friends had survived the explosion, Frank jogged toward the bulldozer. The machine lay on its side next to a smoking black crater.

Frank stared at the black hole until he realized it marked where the silver bomb once stood.

"It wasn't a dud," Frank called back to the others as they trudged toward him.

"That's an understatement," said Bob.

Tommy raised his phone and filmed as Andrew Hepper, thrown fifteen feet from the bulldozer, sat up, covered in dirt and tomato guts.

"I'm going to sue you all," he sputtered.

"You ran a tractor over a bomb, idiot," said Frank, pulling out his phone to call for an ambulance.

"*You* put the bomb there."

"I didn't. T.K. did. Good luck suing a dead man."

Frank and the others continued past Hepper toward the downed plane while the curious crowd followed a hundred feet behind. The hatch creaked open as they approached the crumpled aircraft, and a frail, shaking hand reached out.

"You all gonna shhtand there, or you gonna help me out of thish frickin' plane?"

"Herbert!" Mac grabbed the hand and pulled his friend forward. "You okay?"

The old man clambered out of the crop duster, slapping at his torso and limbs as if checking to be sure they remained attached. "You shsee thoshse tomatoesh exshplode? Jussht like being in the war again." He paused and felt his mouth. "Oh, I think I losshht my teeth. Hold on."

Herbert bent back into the plane and rummaged around the cockpit. After a moment, he appeared again, grinning.

"That's better," he said, gnashing his dentures for all to see.

Mac clapped him on the back. "Where'd you get the tomatoes?"

"Out of T.K.'s storage house in town. Spent half the night fillin' this old plane. Can't you see how swollen my eyes are? Allergic."

The crowd gathered around Herbert, each taking turns to shake his hand.

Bob leaned toward Frank and spoke in a low tone. "You think T.K. got a letter from Hepper and put that bomb out on purpose?"

Frank shook his head. "No telling *this* would happen. I don't think so." He looked away and tried to push down the smile curling up the sides of his mouth.

It was fun to think the bomb had been placed there on purpose.

As the crowd lifted Herbert to their shoulders and carried him toward T.K.'s house, the voice of a child who'd been told the story of The Great Tomato War hundreds of times echoed everyone's only thought.

"The tomatoes really *did* explode!"

CHAPTER TWENTY-TWO

Charlotte pulled to the curb and stared across the street at the home of the people who'd lost and gained a baby—just not the *right* baby. She couldn't imagine their anguish. She'd lose her mind if someone took Abby from her and replaced her with a Bichon Frise. Not that Bichons weren't adorable. She couldn't think about anything except *what's happening to Abby? Is she scared and confused?*

She couldn't imagine someone putting another person through such torment.

Charlotte felt a light pressure on her thigh, as if a tiny forest sprite were strolling across her, and looked down to watch Harley clamber across her lap. The squirrel-sized dog tucked herself between the steering wheel and her belly button.

She had someone else's baby too, but only on loan. Charlotte scooped up little, crazy-haired Harley, stepped outside, and lowered the dog to the pavement to clip the tiny princess' rhinestone-covered pink leash to her collar.

"You're ridiculously small."

Harley scolded her with a sharp yip and waddled off to sniff the grass. Charlotte hustled to keep up with her.

She felt as if she were walking a Teddy bear hamster. *So much different from Abby*. Abby had a neck like a linebacker. That dog could drag her to the end of the block before she could dig heels in deep enough to stop her. Charlotte lamented the lack of dog sleds in Florida—was she keeping Abby from her true calling? Maybe Abby was supposed to be the Rudolph, the Red-Nosed Reindeer of sled dogs, the Wheaten leading a pack of Huskies.

If Harley was a fish on the end of a line, she'd never even know she had a bite.

"This way," cajoled Charlotte, easing the pup in the right direction. She wanted to walk by the house of the unhappy parents, loop around and pass again to see if she saw anything. Siofra could be parked on the block right now, casing the place, watching Charlotte walk her hamster.

She started down the street, Harley trotting beside her, taking seven hundred steps for each of hers, stopping to sniff every few feet like a normal-sized dog. She found it bizarre the doll-like creature acted like *a dog*, though she didn't know how she thought it *would* act.

Charlotte looked up at the sky, worried a hawk or osprey might plunge out of the sun and snatch Harley away. She also wasn't sure what to do when the dog paused other than let it pause. When Abby paused too long and refused to listen to reason, she pulled the leash until the dog relented. With Harley, she was afraid the tiniest tug might pop the miniature Yorkie's head right off her tiny body.

The two of them made their stop-and-go way down the street, past the parked cars where Charlotte hoped to spot someone Siofra-like. No one sat inside any of them. She strolled three blocks past the parents' house and then started back up the street in the opposite direction, Harley never tiring. Any farther away would be too far for anyone to effectively surveil the property.

So terrible.

Her mind drifted to the ways, if faced with a similar situation, she might tell Abby apart from another identical dog. Once, when Abby was young, Mariska had taken her to be groomed, and the dog came back looking like an *alien*. She'd spent a week running Abby through a battery of tests to ensure it was *her*. After that ordeal, she'd even taught the Wheaton a special trick to make sure she would always know the difference—

"Hello."

Charlotte looked up and found the unlucky couple's next-door neighbor staring back at her. A moment earlier, he'd been mowing his lawn. He'd just stopped the engine and now stood wiping his age-speckled brow.

Perfect.

"Hello," she said, pushing her grin to grow. She wanted to look *super*-friendly, hoping to kill two birds with one stone. Sure, she'd wanted to mill around like a random neighbor walking a dog, searching for Siofra watching the house. But as much as solving the baby-napping crime wasn't her *primary* mission, it couldn't hurt to learn more about the case. It *was* interesting. There had to be things the police didn't share with the news because nothing about the case made sense.

Who trades their baby for another?

Her best guess was someone had stolen a baby for another couple looking to gain a child by any means possible. Though that didn't explain the return of a different baby. Did the couple find the first baby lacking and 'returned it to the store for an exchange,' so to speak? Did the kidnapper hope returning the first baby to the parents of the second baby would fool them and keep at least one kidnapping undiscovered?

So bizarre.

Charlotte had given the entire situation much thought, and that scenario was the only one that made sense. The idea of someone giving away their *own* child felt too awful to be a possibility. But to swap one random baby for another...seemed more likely. She hadn't found any local reports of kidnapped babies supporting her theory.

The neighbor stooped over a flower bed to pluck a weed, and his motion drew Charlotte from her thoughts.

He tossed the weed into his lawn, and she could tell he was about to fire up his lawn mower again.

Say something.

"Hey, did they find their baby?" she asked in a more conspiratorial tone. Since the baby swap had already been reported on the news, she hoped her question would make him think she was a neighbor and not a lookie-loo.

Heck, I'm not even reading the news. How could I be up to no good?

The man glanced nervously at the house next door and shook his head. He took a step forward and lowered his voice as well.

"Terrible thing."

"What?"

"They didn't get the baby back."

"What?" asked Charlotte with her best shocked face. "They didn't? Why did I think they did?"

He grimaced. "The police were here all day yesterday. In the end, they were off to get the baby back—"

"Right..."

"—but it wasn't their baby."

Cue even-more-shocked face.

"What? I don't understand."

I'm an idiot. Please tell me everything.

The man sighed. "It was another baby. Not theirs."

"The baby they went to get?"

He nodded, looking as grim as a human could.

Charlotte raised her hand to cover her gaping mouth. "You're *kidding*. The kidnappers returned a different baby? Who does that?"

The man's expression lit as if he'd been waiting all day to share his inside information with someone who hadn't read the paper. "That's what my wife said. She talked to Shana as best she could—the woman was screaming and crying about a *blind* baby."

Charlotte found herself dumbstruck.

A *blind* baby?

The plot thickens.

She scooped up Harley and held the dog close to her. "You're saying someone took their baby and then returned a *blind* baby to them?"

He nodded. "That's what my wife thinks. She said it was all very chaotic, and she thinks Shana was on some kind of sedative." He clucked his tongue. "Leaving her baby on the floor for someone to steal it. *Irresponsible.* I'd leave that woman if I were Carl."

Charlotte recoiled at the man's lack of sympathy, clutching Harley tighter. "I'm sure she never dreamed someone would take him."

He shook his head. "These days, you can never be too careful. She should have known better."

Charlotte took a deep breath.

Now isn't the time to chastise this guy for his lack of empathy.

"Well it's just terrible," she said. "Hey, you didn't see a woman go in there, did you?"

"A woman? Into Carl's house? Who?"

Charlotte paused.

Um...

She didn't exactly know what Siofra looked like at the moment. Before she had to make something up, the old man kept talking.

"I saw a lady cop or two milling around outside while they were waiting for the kidnappers to call."

Charlotte looked away, thinking.

Could Siofra be masquerading as a cop?

Probably not. Too risky.

"No, I was thinking more of a private investigator. Looks like me a little?"

Probably. Maybe. Hard to tell from an old picture and a dubious family connection.

The man tucked back his chin and eyeballed her. "No. I think I'd remember that." He grinned with a set of perfect veneers, and she felt her skin crawl a little.

Ick.

"Ah. Well. I guess we'd better get going." She looked at Harley as if the dog had asked her to get a move on.

The neighbor took a step to the right as if he were trying to block her from leaving, though he stopped short of moving from his yard to the sidewalk. "Which house are you? I haven't seen you before."

"Me? Oh, that one," she said, flicking her finger in the direction she was heading, pointing somewhere in the middle of the street. "I'll see you around."

"See you." He winked.

Not if I see you first.

She hurried away with Harley tucked in her armpit.

Ugh.

He was an old guy with just enough money to think he had a chance with a *much* younger woman. Florida was full of them, though not so much in Charlotte's neighborhood. The modest retirement incomes of the Pineapple Port cruisers kept them in check with the younger ladies. When it came to women their own age, all they had to do was sit back and wait for a hungry widow to find them. The lopsided numbers of men to women placed the men firmly in the catbird seats in Pineapple Port.

Once back in her car, Charlotte set down the dog and tapped her finger against her steering wheel.

That was stupid.

She shouldn't have talked to the man. It would be twice as hard to remain undetected now that someone on the block could recognize her. Certainly, if he spotted her, he'd wonder what she was doing sitting in her car, staring at her neighbor's house.

A careless move, but she *did* get a juicy tidbit of information out of Creepy McNeighbor. *The replacement baby was blind*. The police hadn't released that fact to the press. Someone tried to swap a blind baby for another. That certainly gave her 'defective baby exchange' theory some credence.

Unbelievable.

She'd stopped being shocked by the news years ago, but baby-swapping was even weirder than most stories. If there was one thing the Internet had done besides making case research a *lot* easier, it was to make Charlotte realize how *strange* people could be. She felt as if she could make up any story, no matter how outrageous, and someone out there, *somewhere,* had already done it or, at least, *thought* about doing it.

Terrifying.

Charlotte stared at Shana and Carl Bennett's house. She couldn't see much, thanks to a large hedge wall separating the house from the street. Feeling something wet flick against her forearm, she glanced at Harley. The dog had found a spot curled on the passenger seat, lazily licking Charlotte's hand resting on the center handbrake. Harley seemed tired. The short walk had probably felt like a marathon to little Peewee Muffin-head.

Charlotte peered in her side mirror and watched the neighbor mow his lawn. She didn't want to continue walking to the opposite end of the block until he went inside.

She didn't want to give him any more reason to suspect her of anything.

Instead, she mulled the case. The blind baby information had opened a few more possibilities.

Would someone be willing to trade their own child if it was blind?

The idea was almost unspeakable, but again, she'd read about worse things. Someone might have been that selfish.

But if that's what happened...how do you find the parents of a blind baby?

Maybe those parents hadn't even told anyone their child was blind. If they had and then suddenly had a child who *could* see, they'd have a lot of explaining to do. If they told their friends and family a *miracle* happened, the news could end up online. Who hears about a blind baby with restored vision and doesn't post it on Facebook? People would be *eager* to believe such a happy blessing had occurred. People always believed what they *wanted* to believe. And people loved to share miracles.

But she couldn't sit back and hope Facebook posts would solve the case.

The missing child was six months old, so the blind baby was near the same age. *Did the parents diagnose the blind child's condition themselves?* How do you know a six-month child is blind? It's not like they tossed him a baseball, and he didn't try to catch it—

Charlotte gasped.

A doctor.

Chances were good *somewhere* there was a doctor who'd told those parents their baby was blind. Even if they'd suspected something was wrong, they would have taken the baby to a doctor to confirm those suspicions.

This was a traceable thread. The police needed to find a doctor who'd recently diagnosed a blind baby.

Though, that task might be harder than it sounded. There was no guarantee the baby was local—that might have been the whole point. The parents might have driven or flown from anywhere to enact their kidnapping plan.

But probably not.

This kidnapping didn't seem planned.

The woman who perpetrated the crime had her own baby with her when she stole Shana's—that implied a spur-of-the-moment idea. It had been nothing but luck that she'd parked out of the view of the parking lot cameras.

Probably.

Charlotte caught a movement from the corner of her eye and turned to face the Bennetts' house. She watched two police officers push through the gate. She perked, but as fast as her spine straightened, it curved back down.

Oh no.

What am I doing? I'm supposed to be looking for Siofra.

She realized she wanted to solve the case. But, if she did, Siofra wouldn't have to, and they might miss their chance to spot her.

Hm.

But it wouldn't be right of her *not* to help.

Would it?

Maybe she could just help the police a little.

Scooping up Harley, she left the car and walked to the officers standing on the sidewalk outside the courtyard, one male and one female. She moved quickly to avoid giving herself time to rethink her plan.

"Excuse me," she said.

Two heads turned towards her.

"Yes?" asked the man.

"I've had an idea about the case."

The female officer laughed. "Thanks, but I think we have it covered."

"Are you talking to doctors?"

"Who?" They said in unison, their expressions growing equally grim.

Charlotte suffered a stab of doubt.

Ah well. Too late now.

She plunged ahead.

"Um, I was just thinking it would be a good idea to find the doctor who diagnosed the baby as blind—you probably already thought of that, but—"

"Who told you the baby was blind?" asked the male officer. His badge read *Jackson.*

Charlotte opened her mouth, but nothing came out. She'd forgotten the baby being blind wasn't common knowledge. "Uh, the neighbor, actually. I guess his wife is friends with—"

"Why don't you come inside with us?" asked the female of the pair.

Charlotte put the hand not holding Harley on her chest. "*Me?*"

The female officer nodded. "Sure. You could tell your idea to the captain."

Something about the expressions on the faces of the officers told Charlotte they weren't asking her in because they were *so* impressed with her idea.

They think I'm involved.

She took a step back. "No, it's okay. It was just an idea—"

She started to turn, but the female cop reached out to put a hand on her arm. According to her badge, her name was *Rosey*, but she didn't seem very *rosey* as she glared at Charlotte.

"I'm afraid I'm going to have to insist," said Rosey, making unsettling eye contact with her.

Shoot.

Charlotte could tell she'd passed the point of sweet-talking her way out of her predicament.

"Fine."

She fell into step behind Officer Rosey. Jackson took a spot behind her, no doubt to keep her from running.

CHAPTER TWENTY-THREE

The officers led Charlotte through the hedge gate and into the Bennetts' house. Inside, a woman who appeared near her age stood on her tippy toes in the kitchen, retrieving a plate from a high shelf. Her head turned as the officers entered, and she froze, still on her toes, before lowering to her feet.

"Is that her?" she asked, paling.

The officers shook their heads. "We found her outside. Do you recognize her?"

The pretty woman took a step forward. Charlotte could see every part of Shana *straining* to recognize her as the kidnapper, but after a moment, her body sagged as if someone had released her strings, and she shook her head. "No."

A man appeared from a hallway between the front room and the kitchen.

"Who's this?" he asked. Charlotte assumed he was Carl.

"This woman was outside asking questions about the investigation. Do you recognize her?"

The man shook his head. "No. Should I?"

Charlotte offered the confused couple a smile. They looked as if they hadn't slept in days. Dark circles bagged beneath their eyes. "This is all a misunderstanding. I was just asking your neighbor if the baby had been found yet."

"Is that who told you the baby was blind?" asked Officer Rosey.

Charlotte nodded. "Yes. That's what I was trying to tell you outside—"

"Is that possible?" Rosey frowned at the couple.

"No," said the husband quickly. "You told us not to tell anyone."

He looked at his wife, and she looked away.

"Ask her," suggested Charlotte.

Rosey glared at her, and Charlotte could almost see the words *you shut up* in her eyes. She zipped it.

The officers gazed at the wife, whose eyes pointed towards the floor as if pulled there by a magnet.

"I might have told Judith next door," she mumbled. "By accident."

The husband's face flashed red. "Shana, you weren't supposed to tell anyone—"

"I know, I'm sorry, I just needed to tell *someone,* and it slipped—"

Her husband raised both hands into the air. "So you tell the woman who's married to the biggest busybody on the street?"

Shana's eyes brimmed with tears. "She said she wouldn't tell."

The husband decided to turn his anger on Charlotte. "What are you doing asking around anyway? It's none of your business."

Charlotte felt the eyes of the officers on either side of her burning into her skin. They clearly wanted to know the answer to that same question.

She decided to come clean. "I'm a freelance private investigator. I was trying to help."

Shana took a step forward, the plate still hanging in her hand. "Do you think you can help?"

"All right," said Officer Jackson, motioning for Shana to stop. "We only wanted to see if you recognized her. We'll take her to the station and get this worked out."

"To the station?" peeped Charlotte, her voice growing

pitchy. "But I haven't done anything."

"That's what we're going to figure out," said Jackson, pulling her arm behind her back. Charlotte heard the jingle of cuffs.

"Are you *kidding*?"

"Give me your other hand."

"I can't." Charlotte held up Harley.

Officer Rosey took the dog, and Jackson finished cuffing her. "We'll work this out."

Charlotte huffed. "You could just *ask* me to come. You don't have to *cuff* me." She glanced at Harley, held suspended in the palm of the female officer. "Be careful with her. She's built like a bird."

"I can feel that," muttered Rosey. Charlotte could tell she thought the dog was *ridiculous*.

Probably more of a German Shepherd person.

Jackson urged her towards the door.

Charlotte turned to the couple, still standing in their spots, staring at her.

"Look, I really am a private investigator. I'll try to help."

"No, you won't," said Jackson, irritation dripping from every word.

Shana nodded. "Come back when they're done with you." Her husband looked at her before closing his eyes and rubbing his hand over his balding skull.

CHAPTER TWENTY-FOUR

Hunter watched the officers lead a woman into their patrol car outside the Bennetts' home and lowered her binoculars.

What's that about?

She'd watched the woman pull up in her old Volvo and start walking her dog, a tiny little thing that reminded her of Harley, the dog Angelina owned when she'd left the Inn.

That part had made her smile, but she'd known right away something was up. *That* car didn't belong in *this* neighborhood. And judging by the way the officers were guiding the woman's head into their cruiser, they thought she was off, too.

They didn't seem in a hurry, though. Chances were good that the dog-walking woman wasn't the baby-napper. It could be she was a nosy reporter.

Let's find out.

Hunter grabbed the little notebook sitting on her passenger seat, got out of her Toyota, and moved quickly away from the vehicle. She'd parked five blocks away.

Her car didn't belong in that neighborhood either.

She was also wearing a sheriff's uniform. Cops weren't supposed to arrive in foreign cars they'd won in a poker game on their way from New Hampshire to Florida.

She reminded herself not to let anyone look too closely at her uniform because she'd bought it from a specialized role-play escort service in New York. More specifically, she'd bought it off the hooker they'd sent to her motel room. She didn't want the lap dance, but she *did* want the uniform. She'd given the pale, freckled hooker four hundred dollars and the details of a place upstate she could go if she wanted to leave the life. Hunter suggested leaving with the money she'd overpaid for the uniform would be a good start. So would the window in the motel room's bathroom, allowing the girl to avoid the enormous man waiting in the running Chevy out front. The girl had seemed on the fence until Hunter threw in the keys to her car, also parked out back.

That is why later that evening, she had to insist that stupid college kid put up the keys to his Toyota during the poker game the spoiled brat should never have played.

She paused as she passed the old Volvo in which Yorkie Girl had arrived and jotted down the license plate number in her notepad. She peered inside. Nothing unusual.

Hunter strode to the Bennetts' house and was about to open the gate into the front courtyard when she heard a loud throat-clearing bark from her left.

She stopped and took a step back. The old man that the girl with the Yorkie had been talking to stood on the edge of his property, staring at her.

"Can I help you sir?" she asked, hoping he wouldn't notice her uniform wasn't quite the right style for the area. Or at least she hoped he wouldn't notice the pants were tear-away. That would be a dead giveaway.

"Oh sorry," he said. "It's just you look like an older version of the girl they took away in the police car."

Older. Hm. Thanks for that.

Hunter smiled. "Coincidence."

"Well, *twice* the coincidence," he said as she tried to continue. She stopped and rocked back again.

"Twice?"

He nodded. "She said she was looking for someone who looked something like her. And here you are."

Hunter hung her thumbs in her plastic gun belt and squared up with the man. "You think she was looking for me?"

He shrugged. "Seems like it."

"Did she say why?"

"No. I told her about the blind baby, and she headed right inside there. I guess—"

Hunter held up a palm. "*Blind* baby?"

The man raised his hand to cover his mouth. "Oh, looks like I did it again. You didn't know the baby was blind, either? I keep thinking everyone knows. Especially you folk." He motioned to her uniform.

Hunter shifted, uncomfortable with the critical eye he'd cast on her costume. "The kidnapped one or the returned one?" she asked, moving her hand from her side to her face so he would follow it to her eyes.

"What's that?" he asked as if now, staring at her face, he was talking to a different person.

"Which baby was blind?"

The old man chuckled. "The new one, of course. Who would kidnap a blind baby?"

Hunter grimaced. *Delightful.*

"Well, thank you for letting me know."

"Do you want me to let you know if she comes back? Officer, eh..." He leaned down to squint at her badge. "Firebush?"

Hunter glanced down and realized she'd never looked at the nametag.

The hooker had been a redhead.

"Sure." She reached into her pocket and pulled out her little notebook. Between the pages, she found one of her last remaining cards from her time in New Hampshire and handed it to the man. "You can call me here."

He studied the card, no doubt confused by its simplicity. It wasn't the sort of business card a real officer would have, but she didn't mind the idea of the man alerting her if the girl came back.

"It just says *Hunter*."

"Right. That's my first name."

He shrugged. "Okay."

Hunter nodded and headed back to the gate. She knocked on the door, and the man she assumed was the father of the kidnapped child answered the door.

"Hello, I'm officer—" Hunter winced a little. "—Firebush. They asked me to come and take your statement one more time."

"Everything?" asked the man. "But we've gone over everything a thousand times already."

She softened her expression to show she empathized. "You'd be surprised what comes back to people."

His shoulders slumped. "Fine. Come in."

Hunter nodded and stepped into the home.

CHAPTER TWENTY-FIVE

"Come with me." Angelina crooked her finger in Croix's direction.

Croix looked at her as if she'd come off her tracks, which the smartass girl did three or four times a day, so it didn't slow Angelina for a second.

"What about my post?"

"I'll have Bracco cover it."

Croix blinked at her. "You're kidding."

"What? He'll be fine." She turned to the doorman. "Bracco, watch the desk."

Bracco tipped his cap. "Nightingale."

Croix grimaced and walked from behind her desk to join Angelina at the elevator. They stepped inside, and Angelina used the key around her neck to work the button for the penthouse.

"You need help with Mick?" asked Croix.

"No. Not exactly."

The doors opened, and Angelina strode into the hall and down the corridor until she reached the window at the far westerly side of the building. She tried to open it, pushing, squatting, and grunting until Croix took pity on her, *unlocked the window*, and opened it herself.

Smartass.

Holding out a hand so Croix could steady her, Angelina

stepped through the window and onto the flat part of the roof. Croix followed, squinting in the sun.

"You should have told me to bring my sunglasses," she complained.

"True."

"Why are we on the roof?"

"I want you to look around. Tell me from where you would watch us if you were Siofra."

"You think she's coming *here*?"

"There's a chance."

Croix raised her hands in front of her face and clapped them together in rapid succession. "Ooh, that's exciting."

"Mm-hm."

The girl's expression shifted from glee to confusion. "Why wouldn't she just come through the front door?"

"She might. She also might watch the building from some undisclosed location, and I want to know where that location is before she does."

Croix pursed her lips and walked down the roof line, scanning the area.

"Well, there's the parking lot, of course."

"Duh. We have cameras everywhere for that. Siofra installed half of them. Well, the originals have been upgraded since, but the new installers followed her plan."

Croix swept her finger from left to right as if tracing the Intracoastal waterway behind the hotel.

"She could watch from a boat."

Angelina pulled at her chin. "I thought about that. But the angle isn't good. Especially for seeing into Mick's room."

"So you think she'd be looking for Mick?"

Angelina nodded.

"Hm." Croix looked skyward. "Hot air balloon? F-22A Raptor?"

"Funny. Imagine she doesn't know exactly where he'll be."

"But he's always—" Croix turned. "She doesn't know?"

"No. I don't think so."

"So she'd expect to spot him walking in and out."

"At first."

"But that wouldn't happen."

"Clearly."

Croix turned up her palms. "Well then, this is easy."

"What?"

"Drone. No matter how she decides to surveil the hotel, she won't see Mick walking anywhere, so she'll have to look harder, and there's only one way to look in every window."

"Drone."

"Drone. She could fly one right up here and peek in his window."

"Right. She could use one to watch the hotel too." Angelina grimaced. "How could we track a drone?"

"Well, we couldn't, not really. It would just fly away."

"Could we shoot it with a tracking device?"

Croix traced her toe against the roof shingles, standing on one leg and making Angelina's stomach flip.

"Stand flat! You're making me nervous."

Croix rolled her eyes like a petulant fifteen-year-old. "It's a flat roof. It's no different than standing on pavement."

"It's *different*. Cut it out."

"You're in *heels*."

"Heels are the natural shape of my foot. Cut it *out*."

With a huff, Croix stood on both feet again, but not before circling her arms and pretending she was about to flip off the roof.

Angelina closed her eyes and shook her head.

Smartass young people. I swear I hate them all.

Croix giggled and continued. "I suppose we could hit a drone with a tracker, in theory, but I'd have to see it, get into range, shoot it—all before she flew away."

"That sounds difficult."

"Um yeah. I can't just go buy a tracker-shooting gun on

Amazon. I'd have to build it."

"But you could do that?"

"Sure. But unless I'm perched out here on the roof keeping watch day and night, I'm not sure how I'd spot a drone in time to shoot it."

"But you could do *that*."

Croix frowned. "If you leave Bracco in charge of the front desk that long, we'll lose customers."

Angelina felt a trickle of sweat start down her brow and wiped it away. "Can we get out of the sun? It feels like lasers shooting through my skin."

"You're the one who brought us out here." Croix slipped back through the window and held out a hand to help Angelina back inside.

Angelina steadied herself and then tilted her chin as a brilliant idea smacked her upside her head.

"What if we made it easy?"

"Whaddya mean?"

"What if we left his window uncovered and we set up a gun that we could shoot from anywhere by remote control? A motion-sensing one?"

Croix closed the window and locked it. "You want me to rig a gun that shoots sticky tracking devices at drones outside Mick's window?"

Angelina patted her on the shoulder. "Perfect. Good idea. Make that happen."

Croix sighed, her hands on her hips. "But—"

"Make it happen."

"By when?"

Angelina smiled. "Yesterday." She walked back down the hall toward Mick's room. She tried to look cool because it was important to make the youngster think she *still had it*, but she was so sun-blinded in the relatively dark hall that she nearly clipped her head on a sconce. She thought she heard Croix giggle behind her.

Smartass.

CHAPTER TWENTY-SIX

Angelina took Mick's hand in hers.

"I don't want you to get too excited, but I think Siofra's coming home."

Mick remained still. Of course.

"I know what you're thinking. You're thinking we can't just sit around and wait for her to show up, and I'm here to tell you I have it covered. It's clever. Croix is helping me. We'll find her."

Angelina's phone rang, and she patted Mick's hand before answering.

"Hello?"

"It's Charlotte. Mick's granddaughter."

Angelina rolled her eyes. "I know who you are."

"Right. Good. Because I need you to get me out of jail."

"What?" Angelina's eyes popped wide. "Where's Harley?"

"I have her. They let me keep her."

"In *prison*?"

"I'm in *jail*, not prison. Big difference."

Angelina scowled. "I don't care if you're in the *pokey*. You've got my dog. My baby won't survive in the Big House. She's a gentle princess. Those prison mutts will eat her alive."

She heard Charlotte snort a little laugh.

"They threw me in here while they're waiting for the local sheriff, but I think it might be helpful for me to have a local advocate to vouch for me—"

"Got it. I'm on my way. Don't let anyone turn Harley into their bitch."

Angelina hung up and stood from the chair beside Mick's bed. She kissed his forehead and rubbed the resulting red-lipstick imprint from his skin with her thumb.

"I have to go keep your granddaughter out of prison. Seems your apples land very close to your tree."

Angelina drove to the police station and walked to the reception desk. She'd hoped the regular girl would be there, but she didn't recognize the woman behind the desk.

"I'm here to bail out a little dog."

The woman stared at her, nonplussed. "Just the dog?"

"Maybe."

The woman chuckled. "Well, she doesn't need bailing out. Probably. Palm Beach County sheriff is coming to talk to her, and we were out of waiting rooms."

"Really?"

The woman leaned forward and lowered her voice to a conspiratorial whisper. "No. I just thought it would be funny to put her and her dog in the lockup."

Angelina laughed and glanced at the woman's name tag. "I like your style, Loretta."

The woman beamed. "Thank you."

"But that's my dog."

"Oh." Loretta sighed, her large bosom rising and lowering like a pair of bobbing buoys. "I guess I can let the dog out on good behavior."

"Can I talk to her?"

"The dog?"

"Ha. I see what you did there. The *girl*."

"Sure."

Loretta came around the desk and led Angelina to a pair of cells in the back of the building. Charlotte sat on a bench with Harley tucked under her arm, staring at the ground and stroking the dog with her fingers. She looked up at the sound of their approach.

Loretta opened the door without unlocking it, and Angelina cocked an eyebrow at Charlotte.

"It isn't even locked."

"I didn't say it was."

"Harley," said Angelina, throwing out her hands. Charlotte stood and handed the dog to her.

"This is so embarrassing," said Angelina, taking the dog. "You didn't let her paws touch that dirty floor, did you?"

"That floor is not dirty," mumbled Loretta.

Angelina turned and winked to show she was only kidding. She could tell Loretta was an asset she wanted to keep.

"She's been in my lap the whole time," said Charlotte.

Angelina held Harley in the air, dropping her nose to ping against her own. "Oh my little jailbird. Are you okay? Did mean Aunt Charlotte get you thrown in the clinker?"

Charlotte grimaced. "Why, yes, I'm fine, thanks for asking."

A man with a mustache entered the area from the same door through which Angelina had passed.

"What's going on in here?" he asked.

"Buck!" exclaimed Angelina, as if her long-lost lover had returned from war.

Loretta headed out of the room.

"Nice to meet you, Miss Angelina."

"You too, Loretta."

Angelina followed in her wake until she reached Buck. She threw one arm around him and hugged him sideways to keep Harley from being crushed between them.

"What are you doing back in here?" he asked. "I thought you cleaned up your act."

"Never," she said, playfully poking him in the side.

She turned her head back toward Charlotte and flashed a grin.

I got you, girl.

Chapter Twenty-Seven

Declan heard Bob clear his throat before the man spoke. He closed his eyes to give himself strength.

"Hey, Declan, watcha doin' up there?"

Declan peered down at Bob's upturned face. The rest of him hid behind the roof slant on which Declan perched. He'd climbed up there hoping to fix Charlotte's leak and return to his pawn shop by ten. No one had ever accused him of being a handyman, so his even *greater* wish had been to finish before the old guys in Charlotte's neighborhood noticed him.

He hadn't been on the roof for more than five minutes before the first old shark smelled blood and puttered over to offer advice.

Declan made a conscious effort to unclench his jaw and skootched a little lower on the roofline to get a better view of his audience.

"Hi, Bob. You're up early," he said.

"Not really."

Declan chuckled. "I guess I should say you're *out* early."

Bob shrugged. "If that makes you happier. Whatcha doin' up there?"

"Charlotte's roof leaked right before she left. I thought I'd fix it for her before she got back."

"Oh yeah? Do a lot of roof fixin', do ya?"

"No. Not roofs specifically...but I figured, how hard could it be?"

Bob grunted.

Declan waited a moment to see if Bob would continue peppering him with questions. He clambered back to the spot above Charlotte's bedroom when he didn't. She'd said the drip hit her in the face while sleeping, so the trouble had to be somewhere in that area.

He peeled back a few shingles, but nothing screamed *leak* at him. He'd hoped to find a gaping hole with a little sign next to it that said, "Fix me."

After his initial inspection, Declan turned to see if Bob remained below.

He did.

Bob remained in the same position as before, except his face now tilted toward his watch. As if he felt eyes, he looked back up before Declan could scurry away.

"Doin' it this morning, huh?" asked Bob.

Declan nodded. "Yep. I don't know how long she'll be gone. She might be back today."

"Huh."

The silence deepened between them until Declan couldn't stand it any longer.

"I would have started yesterday, but I had to work."

Bob nodded. "Right. I know all about that."

Declan's brow knit.

Huh?

Bob had been *retired* since he'd known him. Declan opened his mouth to ask him what he meant and then shut it again.

Nope. Don't be an idiot.

Declan spent most of his week talking to his elderly customers, many of whom only came by for conversation. He'd developed a keen sense for when he was about to be tricked into a long, meandering story. The wrong question at the wrong moment could open a never-ending can of worms.

Right now, he sensed he could bait every rod in Florida

with Bob's can of worms.

Declan tried to return to the roof shingles, but the weight of Bob's presence threatened to pull him down the pitch. He glanced back again. Bob had pulled up a porch chair and sat below, staring up at him. Steam rose from the area near his hand.

When did he get a cup of coffee?

Declan scooched back down the roof. "Do you need something, Bob?"

"Nope." He took a sip of his coffee.

Declan grimaced and climbed down his ladder to grab a few tools.

"Need to grab a few things," he said, unsure what else he could say.

"Uh-huh."

Bob tilted a little to the left as if he needed a better view of Declan's tool choices.

"That a steel hammer?" he asked.

Declan looked at the hammer in his hand. "Um, yeah?"

He assumed it was steel. He'd never thought about it.

Why would I?

"Plastic handle or wood?" probed Bob.

Declan looked at the hammer again. "Wood, I think."

"Hm."

Declan looked at him. "Why?"

"Oh, no reason." Bob took a sip of his coffee.

Declan took a deep breath and headed back up the ladder. Already, he wasn't feeling great about his progress. He'd checked inside and found the stain on Charlotte's bedroom ceiling, and then climbed into the attic and spotted where she'd set up a bucket to catch the drip, but he wasn't seeing anything wrong with what he was ninety-nine percent sure was the same spot on the *outside* of the roof. He jerked away another patch of tile and stared with dismay at what looked like a perfectly intact roof.

Maybe I shouldn't have started this.

But what could he do now? He'd already pulled away two dozen tiles. Too late to quit.

"What's he doin' up there?" said a voice.

Declan turned and saw Frank joining Bob in Charlotte's driveway.

Frank looked up at him.

"Whacha doin' up there?"

"Charlotte had a leak. I thought I'd fix it for her before she got back."

"This morning?"

Declan took a deep breath.

Grant me the serenity...

"Yep."

Frank nodded. "Huh."

He walked behind Bob, and Declan heard the sound of an aluminum chair dragging from the back wall of Charlotte's carport. Frank plopped his seat beside Bob and sat down.

Declan stared at them.

You've got to be kidding me.

He returned to his work, tapping with his hammer along the stretch of plywood he'd uncovered.

Maybe I'm not lined up quite right.

He pulled away another tile section with the back of his *steel and wood* hammer.

"What's he doin' up there?"

Declan's head whipped around so fast he almost slid off the roof. He braced his toes to catch himself, clawing at a patch of loose black tiles with his fingers until his momentum ceased.

For a moment, he clung there, panting, and then regained his feet. He peered over his shoulder to see who'd last spoken.

George, the owner of the Pineapple Port retirement community, had joined his rapt audience, and at the sound of Declan nearly falling off the roof, he raised his gaze to stare at him.

"Whoa, Nelly."

Declan's heart still raced. It wasn't a far drop from the gutter to the ground, but it wasn't one he wanted to make, especially with the entire neighborhood watching. He imagined they'd all hold up scorecards to judge his dismount like a bunch of Olympic judges.

"Whatcha doin' up there?" asked George.

"Fixing the roof," muttered Declan as he clambered to his former spot higher up the pitch.

Maybe they wouldn't talk to him if they couldn't see him.

"Started this morning?" asked George, raising his voice.

Declan winced. "Yep."

"Huh."

George took a post standing behind Frank and Bob. He had his own mug of coffee.

Declan tried to focus on the roof.

There must be wood under the wood.

That was it. Some inner seal was leaking. A second layer. He cursed himself for not spending a little more time YouTubing roof-fixing videos. He wanted to pull out his phone, but he *hated* the idea of the three old men catcalling him for using technology. He could hear them now. *"Whatcha doin', Future Boy? Lookin' up how to do it on the Interwebs?"*

It wouldn't end there.

"We never had videos when we were young. When we had to fix something, we just fixed it. We were born knowing how to fix a roof because back then, men were men!"

Declan glanced down at his fan club. He wanted to scream at them he could field-strip an M16 rifle in less than thirty seconds—maybe slightly over blindfolded. The roof confounding him didn't make him less of a man.

Roofs are different.

But that would sound very, very desperate.

Don't let them rattle you.

Somewhere, George found a chair of his own. He guessed it

had been shared by the *other* neighbors who'd shuffled in to join the group because *he* sat in an identical beach chair.

Frank waved. Bob looked at his watch and then smiled up at him.

Sonuva—

Declan stood, and seeing the sheet of plywood he'd uncovered wasn't quite as big as he feared, he stabbed the back of his hammer under the seam and jerked it up. It felt manly, anyway, hearing the nails giving way. Hopefully, he'd earned the approval of his peanut gallery below—

Attic.

Oh no.

All he could see was attic and pink insulation. There was no second leaky layer to explore.

Hm. That's not good.

He glanced down at the group. They blinked back at him.

"Think I found it," he said. He cringed, hating he felt the need to lie.

"That's good," said Bob.

"Any minute," said Frank.

Declan frowned.

Did Frank say, 'any minute?' What did that mean?

A gust of wind caught Declan off-guard, and he threw out his hands to catch his balance. His grip loosened on the hunk of plywood, and it snapped back into place, dislodging a chunk of roof tiles, which slid down the roof, teetered in the gutter for a second then tumbled to the ground not far from the men gathered below.

"Sorry," called Declan as he dropped to his butt, head low enough that the men couldn't make eye contact with him anymore.

Something about the skyline caught his attention.

Is it getting darker?

He'd come out at first light, assuming it would get easier to see as time ticked by. But now, it felt as though—

For the first time, he saw the deep, gray storm clouds headed his way. Another gust of wind ruffled his hair, and he heard the low rumble of thunder.

A storm was coming fast.

Declan heard a scraping noise and stood to stare down at the men. They folded up their chairs. Frank and Bob disappeared beneath the carport to return their seats to their places. The neighbor Declan didn't know was already half way across the street, a beach chair tucked under each arm. George pointed toward home.

Bob reappeared and looked up at him, grinning.

"Did you know there was a storm coming?" asked Declan.

Frank walked by and waved without looking at him.

"Yep," said Bob.

"You all did?"

"Yep."

The wind whipped up again, and Declan had to lower his hands to the roof, his butt in the air, like the backend of a horse costume, sans costume.

"None of you thought it might be nice to tell me?" he called over the grumble of thunder.

The world grew even darker.

"What?" asked Bob.

"I said none of you told me a storm was coming!" The first of the rain pelted his skin.

Nearly across the street and a few steps from his own safe, dry home, Bob turned and grinned, waving. He cupped his hands around his mouth.

"What fun would that be?"

CHAPTER TWENTY-EIGHT

"Thank you for getting me out of jail."

It was four o'clock, and the sun still shone enough to keep the biting mosquitos and no-see-ums at bay. Charlotte offered Angelina a sheepish smile from her rocking chair overlooking the Intracoastal waterway behind the hotel. To their right, a large swath of preserved land served as home to the pair of osprey circling above them, both searching for an afternoon snack swimming through the water below.

Angelina sat in her rocking chair with Harley curled on her lap. The hotel concierge-slash-woman-of-mystery seemed pensive, which, for the short time Charlotte had known her, didn't seem to be one of her more common emotions.

Charlotte chalked it up to Siofra's potential return. Or maybe Angelina always sat on the back porch at the end of the day and watched the sun dip below the palm trees. She hoped the woman wasn't mad at *her*. Had she overstepped a boundary asking for help with the police? Should she get her a thanks-for-keeping-me-out-of-prison gift? What was the perfect present for the woman who sweet-talked you out of jail time?

Do they have a Hallmark card for this?

Angelina's head snapped up as if Charlotte had just finished speaking, though it had been a minute or two. "No problem. I don't usually have to bail out people until the third or fourth date, but my pleasure."

Charlotte snickered. Angelina's mind had clearly been elsewhere; she didn't seem angry at her. The woman's joke repeated in her head, and the second time around, one of the words struck Charlotte as odd.

"Wait, you didn't actually have to bail me out, did you?" she asked.

Angelina shook her head. "No. You weren't officially arrested."

Charlotte put her hand on her chest. "Whew. I didn't think so."

"Anyway, it isn't me you have to apologize to. It's Harley." Angelina tussled the wild crop of hair sprouting from Harley's head. "That ordeal was beneath her dignity."

Charlotte leaned down to get eye level with the dog. "That's true. I apologize, Harley." At the sound of her name, the Yorkie opened the glistening black pools she used for eyes to peer at Charlotte and then shut them again.

Charlotte leaned back in her rocking chair. "What a mess. They shouldn't have taken me to the station. They didn't like that I knew the baby was blind, but—" She raised a hand to her mouth. "Whoops. I probably wasn't supposed to say that."

Angelina turned. "What baby is blind?"

"The one returned to the couple."

"The kidnappers replaced their baby with a *blind* one?"

Charlotte nodded. "Puts a whole new spin on the kidnapping, doesn't it?"

Angelina clucked her tongue. "I don't know what's going on in the world today. Everyone is crazy."

Charlotte glanced at her watch. "I'm going to go give my boyfriend a call. He's probably wondering if I've run off to Australia by now."

"A country originally colonized by English prisoners. Your kind of folk."

Charlotte laughed. "You're never going to let me live this down, are you?"

Angelina grinned. "Nope." She stood, and Harley grunted her displeasure at being tucked into the crook of her mama's arm when she'd had a perfectly good lap on which to sleep.

Charlotte wandered off the porch and down the path leading to the centermost dock to find a perch at the end of it. Feet dangling over the water, she dialed Declan.

He answered on the third ring. Instead of hearing the soothing sounds of the sixties in the background, what sounded like the squeal of an electric saw accosted her ears.

"Declan?"

"Hey, hi. How are you?" he asked, sounding flustered. The grinding noise stopped.

"Are you okay? What's going on?"

"Hm? Nothing. They're doing some construction next door."

"You're outside?"

"Hm? Oh. Yep. What's up?"

"Oh. Things have gotten complicated here." She paused, weighing the pros and cons of sharing her trip to jail, and decided to come clean. "I spent the day in jail."

"What? Did you say *jail*?" he asked as the sound of a saw pealed again.

"Yes, but it was a misunderstanding. My aunt might return to this area to look into a missing baby case. It's crazy. Someone stole someone's baby and replaced it with a blind one."

"Uh-huh."

Charlotte didn't feel *uh-huh* was the appropriate response to her news. The construction had to be getting to him.

"How about I call you later when you're home, and it's quiet?"

"Right."

"Right, what?"

"Right, uh..." Declan paused. "I'm not sure. I'm sorry. I'm a little distracted—"

"I can tell. That's why I said I'll call you later."

"Oh. Yep. That would be better. It's crazy noisy here."

"Yep. Okay, so I'll talk to you—"

"Hey, can I ask you a quick question first?"

Charlotte watched the osprey dive. "Sure. It's not noisy over here." *Quite the opposite.* The place was tranquility personified. "I can't promise you'll hear my answer, though."

"I'll put my finger in my other ear. Do old men check the weather every morning?"

"What?" As promised, Charlotte heard every word he said, but the question didn't make a lot of sense.

"I said, do all old men check the weather in the morning? Is it a thing?"

Charlotte laughed. "Yes. It's like a full-time job after retirement. Especially in Florida, where it changes every five minutes."

Declan made a noise that sounded something like a growl and a grunt had a baby.

"Why?" she asked.

The saw wailed again as a hammer sang backup.

"Nothing. I'll talk to you later. Be careful. Love you."

"Love you, too."

Charlotte hung up and leaned back on her hands to watch a paddle-boarder paddle by. She waved, and the woman waved back.

She closed her eyes and tilted her head to catch the last of the day's winter sun.

Now she had three mysteries to solve. The location of her mysterious aunt, the location of the missing baby, and what the heck Declan was up to.

CHAPTER TWENTY-NINE

Kim watched Josh bounce the fussy baby on his knee.

Their baby might have been blind, but this child was *fussy*.

No.

Worse than fussy. He was some sort of demon child.

I am being punished.

There was no doubt of that.

Josh Jr. had been sweet. She could tell he had a really good heart. And, most of all, he'd been *her* baby.

She felt the tears welling up in her eyes for the hundredth time and turned so her husband wouldn't see.

"What's wrong with you?" asked Josh.

She sniffed and wiped her eyes. "Nothin'. Hormones."

Josh shook his head and handed the baby to her. "I don't know what's wrong with him. All he does is cry now."

She bounced Josh Jr. up and down against her chest to get him to settle.

Except it isn't Josh Jr., is it? You terrible, terrible woman.

She walked to the window to turn her back to Josh.

Why did I do it? What was going through my head?

It was a mistake. She knew that now. She didn't want this woman's devil baby. She wanted *her* baby. It didn't matter that he was blind. Josh would just have to *deal*.

She turned and glared at the side of her husband's head as he watched ESPN, beer in hand.

This is all his fault.

It didn't matter that Josh Jr. couldn't see. She would have *never* traded her baby for another if she hadn't been so terrified of her husband finding out his precious sports-star son was less than perfect.

What now?

Josh looked at her as if he'd felt her hate burning into the side of his face. "Can you shut him up or take him—" His frown deepened. "What're you lookin' at?"

"Nothin'," she muttered. She headed toward the bedroom.

"I swear, you're like a crazy woman lately," she heard him call as she left.

She flipped the door shut behind her and sat on the edge of the bed to bounce the baby on her knee. She stared at him as if he were an alien with her teeth clamped so tight her jaw began to hurt.

I want my baby back.

CHAPTER THIRTY

Hunter made a looping arc to head the opposite way on her paddleboard. She saw the young woman at the end of the dock, apparently still on her phone call.

Here we go.

She knew when she saw Angelina gather the girl from jail that she'd have to talk to her. How did this girl know Angelina? What were the chances someone staying at the Loggerhead Inn would be involved in the case *she* came to solve?

Life was starting to get *pushy*. It'd felt like a sign when she saw the missing baby case happened in Jupiter Beach. Or, maybe she forced herself to believe the universe was sending her a message. Swapped babies weren't *quite* the case she usually sank her teeth into.

But now, to have someone from the hotel involved...

The universe was getting a little heavy-handed.

She looked up at the blue sky.

I'll go home when I'm ready, dammit—

The girl lowered her phone but remained sitting on the edge of the dock, her legs kicking back and forth over the water. Head tilted back and eyes closed, she stayed there until Hunter cruised within twenty feet. Although she'd tried hard not to make a sound, the girl sensed her. Her eyes popped open, and her face pointed in Hunter's direction as if an alarm had gone off.

"Hi again," said the girl.

Behind her glasses, Hunter glanced at the Inn behind the girl, the shape of it so familiar it felt like an old friend.

It's weird to see you again.

She tried to say *hi*, but the word stuck in her throat. She cleared it and tried again.

"Hi."

The girl motioned to the paddleboard. "Is that hard? I've never tried it."

Hunter glided to the dock's piling, resting her hand on it for balance and anchoring herself in the moving water.

"Just a matter of balance and practice. Are you staying here? Is it nice?"

The girl chuckled. "Little strange, but nice."

Hunter watched a great blue heron pick its way along the opposite bank, chewing at her lip as she tried to decide how she wanted to initiate her interaction with the stranger. She could coax information out of her, revealing nothing about herself, or she could come at her head on, asking what she most wanted to know and maybe reveal a little about herself.

What she revealed would be lies, of course. She might have to throw in a few half-truths.

Ah, what the heck.

"I guess they must be nice people. I can't remember when a hotel manager got me out of jail."

The girl's smile dropped so fast Hunter thought she heard it splash into the water.

"Who are you?" she asked.

"Hunter." She held out a hand, and the girl paused before shaking it.

"Charlotte. How did you—"

Hunter choked on a bit of spit.

"Are you okay?" asked the girl.

She nodded. "How do you know Angelina?" Hunter looked away to hide her wince. She was only two sentences into her conversation, and she'd already made it clear *she* knew Angelina.

Sound a little eager, why don't you?

Angelina's name felt funny in her mouth.

Slow down. You're revealing too much.

Charlotte shut her mouth and seemed to come to terms with the fact her question had been deflected. She glanced back at the Loggerhead Inn as if it would tell her the answer Hunter needed. "I don't *know* her. Not really. We just met yesterday."

Hunter frowned, unsure if she believed the girl. "Why would she get you out of jail if you don't know each other?"

Charlotte leaned forward on the dock, squinting at her. Studying her.

She's no shrinking violet.

"How do you know I was in jail today? And how do *you* know Angelina?"

Hunter shrugged. "I've known her longer than you, so I get to ask the questions."

She forced a chuckle. She'd said the words to avoid the question in a light, humorous way, but to her ear, the phrase sounded like a petulant four-year-old making up rules to her own game. She had to be nicer, or she wouldn't find out what this stranger knew about the baby case *or* the people at Loggerhead. She had to know something, or the cops wouldn't have taken her away in a squad car, and Angelina wouldn't have broken her out of jail.

Be nice.

Hunter grinned. "Just kidding. When the police took you away, I followed. I'm a private detective working for the parents of the kidnapped child."

There you go. Nice. Helpful. See how easy that was?

"You are?" Charlotte's eyes opened wide. "So am I."

"You're working with the parents?"

"No. Sorry. I'm a detective, and I was *hoping* to help the parents, but the police decided they wanted to take me away for questioning before I had a chance to make my *case*, so to speak."

Hunter glanced at the hotel, hoping to see movement. It looked the same as the last time she'd been there. Maybe the landscaping was different; she didn't remember all the crotons. She scanned the spots where she'd installed cameras and saw similar, updated technology still occupying the locations she could see. One camera trained on the dock. She tucked herself behind the piling to avoid its gaze.

Hunter rocked side-to-side on the paddleboard, trying to appear as loose and easy-breezy as possible as she refocused on Charlotte.

Don't be suspicious, Charlotte. I'm like a goofy, friendly Labrador. Pay no attention to the man behind the curtain.

"So you didn't say why Angelina bailed you out?"

A bit of a blush rose to Charlotte's cheeks. "Oh, she didn't have to bail me out. I wasn't officially arrested. They just wanted to make sure I wasn't up to anything. You know."

"Why would they jump to that conclusion?"

"I knew the baby was blind."

Hunter tilted her head. "Did you? That wasn't shared with the press."

I know that now.

Charlotte nodded. "The neighbor spilled the beans about two seconds before I knocked on the door."

"Ah."

Charlotte shielded her eyes from the setting sun to watch the blue heron stab at a fish.

"So how did you know they arrested me?"

Hunter smiled.

She's trying to look casual, too.

I like this girl.

"I saw Angelina at the police station with you. I was talking to them about the case."

"Oh."

Charlotte swung her legs back and forth, looking wistful. "I meant well. I suggested they find the doctor who diagnosed the blind baby and trace him or her back to the parents."

Hunter, who had been watching the water flow along the sides of her board, looked up.

Hey, that was my idea.

"There has to be an official criminal inquiry, and they need a court order to make the doctors break confidentiality," she said. It was true. She'd already looked into it.

Charlotte nodded. "I know. Though—"

Hunter looked at her expectantly.

She's wondering if she should share her ideas with me.

"Why don't we work together?" Hunter blurted.

Why did I say that?

She looked at the hotel again.

That's why. She's my key to the Loggerhead. My inside man.

Hunter released a sigh. Just once, she wished she could have a little patience instead of pushing for information as fast as she decided she wanted it.

Charlotte shook her head. "I don't want to step on your toes."

"Oh, you wouldn't be. My, uh, assistant is sick, and I could use the help."

"Really? That's a shame. Nothing serious, I hope?"

Hunter was still staring at the Loggerhead and said the first thing that came to mind. "Shingles."

"Yikes. I hear that's painful."

Hunter blinked at her. She had no idea what *shingles* were exactly. She'd just been staring at the side of the hotel when Charlotte asked. Something to do with chickenpox? She decided to nod her head grimly.

"Right. So I'll split the money with you since you're a full-blown detective already."

"Really? You don't have to—"

"No, it's fine."

Half of nothing is nothing.

Hunter continued, feeling better about her decision. Her plan to bring Charlotte into her fake employ would also keep the girl from meddling in her case. "So what were you thinking about the doctors?"

"Oh, I was thinking I could maybe work the nurses. One of them might cough up information about tragic diagnoses without realizing—"

"Especially if they heard it was about this case."

Charlotte perked and pointed at her. "Right. It's all over the news."

"But where would you start? There are multiple hospitals and private practices—assuming the kidnapper even lives in this area."

"I think she does. It didn't seem planned. I think she did it on a whim."

Hunter nodded. *Agreed.* "I think I can narrow things down a little."

"Yeah?"

"Brody was wearing a Burberry jumper. The swapped baby returned wearing a brand *much* more affordable."

"So they didn't even try to *sell* the new baby by putting him in the original's clothes? They kept the expensive jumper."

"Yep. I don't think our baby-napper has much money."

"No. So maybe not a private practice. A hospital. Maybe even an emergency room."

"That's what I'm thinking. I'm also thinking she might be regretting the kidnapping by now."

Charlotte nodded. "You'd think so. Unless this is some kind of messed up adoption scam."

Hunter nodded. "Maybe one of us could stake out the home to see if the napper drives by mulling a swap-back. The other can try the doctor idea."

Charlotte smiled. "I'm game."

"Great." Hunter fished her phone from the waterproof case strapped on her arm and then shook her head. "Give me your phone. I'll put in my number."

Charlotte hesitated and then handed her the phone. Hunter pretended to be fascinated by something on her own phone while she sent a request to Charlotte's phone to allow herself access to *find location*. Then she shifted to Charlotte's phone, accepted the request, and saved herself as a contact.

"Here you go. I'm a contact now. I'll give you a call tomorrow morning?"

Charlotte took the phone and shrugged. "Sure. Great."

Hunter picked a splinter from the piling and dropped it into the water. "So, you just met Angelina? Is she still dating that guy at the hotel?"

Charlotte scowled. "I don't know. Who?"

Hunter shrugged. "I don't remember his name."

Shea. Mick. Dad.

Charlotte shook her head. "I don't know. Like I said, I just met her."

"Right. No biggie."

Aaaand...subject change.

"So you're a *local* detective?" asked Hunter.

Charlotte shook her head. "No. Other side of the state."

"But you love working on kidnapped baby cases so much you came here?"

Charlotte laughed. "No. It was a family thing. Long story. Turns out my grandfather owns the hotel." Charlotte hooked a thumb back at the building.

Hunter felt her face grow tingly.

What?

"Last I heard, Mick McQueen still owned this place," she said, her words barely audible.

Charlotte heard. "Yep. That's him."

Hunter swallowed. "Mick's your grandfather?"

"As it turns out."

"You're Grace's kid?"

Charlotte perked. "Yes. Did you know her?"

Hunter shook her head and pushed off the piling. "Not really. Well, I better get going."

Charlotte stood and brushed off her posterior. "Do you want to come in and say hi to Angelina?"

"Hm?"

No. I want to run away. Now. Too much to think about.

"No. I don't even know if she'd remember me. I better get back to work." She paused a moment before her paddle broke the water and lifted it to point it at the Loggerhead. "Is Mick there?"

Charlotte nodded and pointed a finger at the top of the hotel. "Yep. He's up there."

Hunter looked at the penthouse windows.

He's there.

"Okay. Text me your number."

"Will do."

Hunter paddled as hard as she could without looking like a crazy person.

How did Grace's kid find out about this place?

She paddled to the waterfront home from where she'd stolen the paddleboard and dragged it onto the dock. A landscaper trimming the hedges of the multi-million dollar property glanced at her as she walked up the dock and headed for her car. He smiled and looked away. She wasn't worried about him. He wouldn't alert the owners to her presence, especially if she looked as if she belonged there, which she did. It helped that she was older now. If she were twenty, he might think she was a kid up to no good, but no one thinks a woman in her forties is running around appropriating paddleboards. She could let herself in the back door and have a muffin, and no one would think it was odd, even though they'd never seen her at the house before.

Of course, when she was *twenty*, she had other assets to distract people.

It all evened out. You lost youth. You gained wisdom.

Hopefully.

She wondered sometimes.

As Hunter reached the car she'd parked in front of the waterfront mansion, she didn't feel wise.

Mick was there.

He's up there.

She sat in the driver's seat without turning on the car, staring through the window at nothing but the thoughts swirling in her head.

He's up there.

What did Charlotte mean by that? How would she know he was in a particular spot of the hotel at *that* moment? Mick wasn't the kind of guy who held still for very long. Except for that time he had food poisoning—

Is he sick? Is that how she knew exactly where he was?

She turned on the car.

Maybe I'm reading too much into it.

Maybe.

CHAPTER THIRTY-ONE

Kim tucked the baby into the car seat and sat behind the wheel. The baby screamed to be released. It reminded her of when her high school boyfriend practiced with his band, and she'd perch in front of the speakers to show her support.

No way to get away from the noise.

She twisted in her seat and raised her voice over the din.

"Please stop. Please? We're just going shopping, and then we'll go home and—"

Her voice crumbled, pounded to dust by the baby's wailing. Placing a hand over each ear, she turned and rested her forehead on the steering wheel. A tear slid down her nose and into her lap.

This is my punishment.

A line she'd heard in church echoed in her head.

You reap what you sow.

How did it go? Something about sowing your sinful nature meant you'd reap destruction. She remembered asking her mother why sewing was bad, and her mother laughed.

Kim's stomach lurched at the thought of her mother discovering what she'd done.

She'll know. She'll know he isn't Josh Jr.

A silence settled in the minivan, and she peered into the rearview mirror. Behind her, the baby, still red-faced from his fit, gnawed on his fist.

Thank you.

She turned the key, and the engine roared to life.

The baby shrieked a single note that felt like an icepick through the back of Kim's head.

Her knuckles turned white on the wheel.

I'm reaping what I sowed.

The baby wanted to go home. If she'd thought about the consequences of her kidnapping another woman's baby, which she hadn't, she would have realized the baby himself might have something to say about being torn from his mother.

The lack of information in the paper about the baby swap ate at her night and day. Why didn't they talk about Josh Jr.? Where was he? They'd reported the baby returned wasn't Brody Bennett, but then *nothing*. Did they know he was blind? Mrs. Bennett looked rich. Her baby's clothes were worth more than every stitch of clothing Josh Jr. owned.

Maybe that woman could find a doctor to fix Josh Jr.—in Sweden or something? She'd heard about rich people finding solutions in other countries. She'd fed herself that thought a thousand times in the last few days, trying to convince herself Josh Jr. was better off in his new home.

Kim started driving. She pushed her hand into her pocket at the first traffic light and pulled out a crumpled paper.

She'd written down the couple's name and address. *Shana and Carl Bennett.* She'd done a few Internet searches and found their house easily enough. They lived on the beach. Well, not *on* the beach, but a heck of a lot closer than she did.

Josh Jr. would have a better life with them.

Oh no.

A thought hit her so hard it felt like a knife stabbed into her belly.

What if they didn't keep Josh Jr.?

What if they weren't even *allowed* to keep him?

The baby behind her found a new gear and screamed at a higher pitch.

No, no, no...

She'd felt a little ill when she read in the paper the Bennetts knew Josh Jr. wasn't their baby. As long as they didn't *know*, a window remained for her to think. She'd imagined scenarios where she stole Josh Jr. back and replaced him with their awful baby. No one would even know. When that window closed, she kept from losing her mind by telling herself Josh Jr. would be better off with the rich couple.

But what if they didn't keep him?

What if the police put him in an orphanage?

A horn blared. Kim jumped, startled to hear something louder than Brody Bennett.

Green light.

She hit the gas. She traveled another quarter mile in a daze and stopped at the next light, for once, happy to hit the light. It gave her time to think. The baby settled into quiet, wet sniffles as if he wanted her to think, too.

Josh Jr. in an orphanage.

She couldn't let that happen.

Kim perked as a thought lighter than the dark notions roiling in her brain bobbed to the surface.

I could adopt him back.

Maybe no one would want a blind baby, and *she* could adopt him?

No sooner had her spine straightened with this buoying thought than her shoulders hunched again.

No. Josh would never allow her to adopt someone else's baby. Not when he was happy making his own kids. And they wouldn't pass the financial hurdles adoptive parents no doubt had to clear. Not to mention the *inspections*. The State only had to spot the fist-sized hole in the living room wall to know Josh couldn't deal with another screaming child. He'd been staying at the bar even later since she brought home wailing Brody Bennett.

They'd put Josh Jr. in an orphanage, and another couple'd

adopt him. They could be anyone. They'd probably be kind if they were the sort of people to adopt a blind baby in the first place. But they might move him clear across the country. They might be hiding how horrible they really are. They might be devil-worshippers for all she knew, looking for a cheap baby to sacrifice—

Kim stomped on the gas and made an abrupt turn in front of the car sitting next to her at the light. The driver hit the brakes and horn, but she barreled on, heading for the bridge that led to the beach.

I have to see Joshy. I have to get him back.

At the next light, she fumbled for her phone and plugged in the address she'd scrawled on that scrap of paper. She knew the way. The streets weren't difficult to navigate once you were on the island— there weren't that many of them.

Kim drove over the bridge and turned onto the street where the Bennetts lived. She slowed the moment she made the left so it wouldn't look strange when she slowed in front of the Bennetts' house. Thanks to the hedge wall, she couldn't see much, but the low, decorative gate had the right numbers bolted to its bars. She passed a few parked cars, her eyes locked on the police cruiser outside the address.

She strained, trying to see *anything*. No officers sat in the cruiser.

They had to be inside.

Give me a glimpse. Give me a peek at Josh Jr. to let me know he's there and he's alright.

As her minivan crept past the house, Brody screamed.

Kim almost jerked the wheel directly into the police cruiser. Panicked, she hit the gas and passed the house.

She drove a few streets away and pulled to the curb, sobbing.

"Why? Why couldn't you just let me see if he was there?" she screamed at the baby behind her.

Brody settled. When she turned, she could have sworn he

was smiling.

　　Kim swallowed.

　　You're the angel of revenge.

CHAPTER THIRTY-TWO

Charlotte heard a rattling noise and opened her eyes. The room was dark, and it took her a moment to realize where she was.

Loggerhead Inn. Right.

Her legs curled like question marks to make room for a sleeping dog not there, and then she stretched to give her knees a break. A peek at her watch told her it was three-thirty in the morning.

She groaned. Way too early to wake.

No wonder I feel like my brain is full of wadded paper towels.

Wiping the sleep from her eyes, she sat up.

Something felt different. Something *different* had woken her. Over the past two nights, she'd heard boats motoring down the Intracoastal and the occasional whistle of what she guessed was some sort of cargo train, but something about this awakening felt different.

Beside her, her phone glowed.

Ah. Phone.

She picked it up and saw two texts from the mysterious Hunter.

Hunter, my butt.

The woman on the paddleboard was *Siofra.*

She felt it in the very marrow of her bones.

Though the only photo she'd ever seen of Siofra hailed from two decades earlier, the woman bore an uncanny resemblance to her own mother, whom she'd *seen* in her forties.

Besides, who else would work the baby-napping case *and* case the Inn?

Hunter was a striking beauty, even with her long dark hair pulled into a ponytail and not a pat of makeup on her face. Still, the lines near her eyes told Charlotte she had to be at least forty-five, which put her at the right age. She was in great shape, though. As she'd paddled away, Charlotte had watched the muscles in her arms and back flex.

She had to be some sort of athlete.

Did she run away to join the Olympic team?

It had *killed* Charlotte to be unable to burst into the Inn and tell Angelina she thought she'd met Siofra. For one, Angelina was the only person—well, the only *conscious* person—who could positively identify her. But another nugget kept her from telling Angelina all.

She found it odd Hunter had chosen to talk to her. Why would she risk her cover?

Did she know I'm her niece before I told her? Or was it a coincidence?

And now here the woman was again, texting her pre-dawn.

Almost pushy.

Charlotte needed time to discover what Hunter was up to without Angelina scaring her away. She didn't feel Angelina could sit tight and keep her mouth shut. If Hunter was as savvy as Angelina implied, Charlotte guessed her aunt would be long gone before Angelina caught her.

Charlotte took a moment to silently vow to let Angelina know about 'Hunter' *before* Siofra went missing again.

I'll tell her today.

Maybe tomorrow.

Charlotte read Hunter's first text.

I'm doing the hospital search.

Huh? Now? She's decided three-thirty a.m. was a great time to grill nurses for information about a blind baby?

I guess hospitals are open twenty-four-seven.

Apparently, so were Hunter's eyes.

Maybe early *was* a good time to talk to the nurses. They'd either be tired from a long shift or tired from waking up too early. They might be happy to talk about something other than late-night trauma victims or the long work day ahead of them.

Or maybe Hunter was just an early riser and had already started planning her day.

Charlotte read the next text.

That means you do the surveillance.

She frowned. And just like that, Hunter was her boss, assigning her a job for the day. They'd discussed two plans, and somehow she'd drawn the short stick.

How come she gets to do the fun thing, and I have to watch the Bennetts' house for regretful kidnappers?

Charlotte looked at her watch again. Does she mean now? Would the kidnapper drive by the house at night?

Maybe. If the napper couldn't sleep, ruing the day she'd swapped her child for another. *Though, at night, she wouldn't be able to see much... Should I start now?*

The phone buzzed in her hand to announce another message from Hunter.

I'd start now.

Charlotte huffed and considered several reply text versions before punching in four letters and a period.

On it.

Hunter was much too cool. She wanted to keep it short. She didn't want to be all, *Sure, Hunter, whatever you say! I'm on the case! Smiley-face, smiley-face, thumbs up, unicorn, rainbow!* and come off like a huge dork.

No sooner did she send it than she regretted it.

I should have said, "Fine."

That would have implied she didn't appreciate having her assignments picked, too.

Ah, the nuances of text.

Charlotte waited a moment to see if any more texts came in and realized she was acting like a teenager waiting for her boyfriend to call back and put the phone down.

Be cool.

She showered and dressed and checked the phone again. Nothing. Apparently, Hunter had delivered her message and moved on with her life.

Like a cool person.

Charlotte sighed.

Maybe, someday, I'll be cool.

CHAPTER THIRTY-THREE

Hunter picked through the pile of books sitting on the seat beside her, noting the name of the second-hand bookstore stamped on the inside covers. Jana DeLeon, Janet Evanovich, Kathi Daley, Julie Smith—apparently, the vehicle owner liked mysteries. Too bad now *she* had to crack the case of why this woman didn't have an extra set of scrubs in her car.

She'd thought for *sure* the older nurse she'd watched leave the vehicle would have a spare set of scrubs in the trunk somewhere. Didn't nurses always carry a change of clothes? They never knew who might bleed or barf on them. And this woman had a particular taste. The scrubs she'd been wearing had tiny wiener dogs wearing party hats scattered all over them. No way she'd be happy changing into a plain blue or green set provided by the hospital. Perish the thought.

But nope. No spare wiener dogs. Not even cats.

Hunter had thought she'd hit the lottery when the woman failed to lock her door. Someone whose clothes implied she had a penchant for carrying spare outfits, an unlocked door... How *dare* the universe align all the planets just to skip Pluto?

I guess Pluto is a bit of a red-headed stepchild these days.

Didn't the space scientists declare it *not* a planet?

Ah well.

Nurse Pluto didn't have a change of clothes. Just a pile of well-creased books from a second-hand bookstore.

Hunter watched another car enter and park from her new seat in Nurse Pluto's car in the employee parking lot. A man in scrubs exited an old Honda and headed for the hospital.

Hm. A man. Men were less likely to think ahead, but she'd give it a shot. She didn't have to worry about alarms with an older car, so there was no reason not to try.

Hunter exited the mystery reader's car and moved to the man's vehicle. He'd left the windows cracked far enough that she could snake her arm inside, but she came up short of releasing the lock. She grunted and leaned farther inside. Something snapped, and the window dropped another inch.

Whoops.

She opened the car and sat inside. Stretching back, she grabbed a backpack from the backseat and pulled it to her.

Voila. Among the protein bars and running clothes, there was a spare set of scrubs.

Hunter pulled them out and slipped into the top. The collar of her tank plunged deep enough she didn't need to remove it. Stepping out of the car, she gave the area a visual sweep and dropped her shorts to the ground to don the scrub pants.

Not bad.

They fit pretty well, considering. She was tall, and the car's owner wasn't, so the pant bottoms didn't drag on the ground. Hunter stashed her shorts inside a flowering shrub sprouting from a planter-slash-retaining-wall in front of the car. She took one step toward the hospital before stopping to stare at the collapsed window of the Honda.

Shoot.

Poor guy. A working nurse with such an old car. It was criminal what they paid nurses in Florida, and now here she was, vandalizing the guy's car.

Maybe it's not *really* broken.

It was hard to tell *how* broken the window might be without turning the car over.

Hunter returned to her shorts and peeled three hundred

dollar bills from her pocket. Thinking better of leaving her cash in a planter, she tucked the remaining wad into her shelf bra and stuffed the shorts back into the shrubbery. Slipping her hand through the fallen driver's-side window, she dropped the bills onto the car's front seat.

She took a few steps away, thought better of it, and returned. If she left hundred dollar bills on the seat, the car might be even *more* ransacked by the time the guy clocked out. She tucked the money in the ashtray and tried once more to head for the hospital.

One point for good karma.

Hunter checked the directory in the lobby and headed for the pediatric unit. Even if the mother of the blind baby brought the child to the emergency room, one of the pediatric doctors would have examined it.

She strolled by the desk where an administrative woman typed on a computer.

Hunter leaned against the desk. "Whew, what a night."

The woman looked up and smiled. "Just getting off?"

Hunter nodded. "Pretty soon. Had to tie up some loose ends."

The woman nodded and returned to her work.

"Hey, where can I find the doctor who diagnosed that blind baby a while back?"

The woman looked up again.

"What's that?"

"I, um, accidentally took home some paperwork on a blind baby, and now I forget which doctor handed it to me."

The woman scowled. "The doctor's name isn't on it?"

"No. Weird."

"Let me see it."

Hunter slapped at pockets she didn't have. "Oh, I left it in my car..."

The woman sighed. "I don't remember anyone diagnosing a blind baby."

Another nurse walked behind the desk area, and Hunter recognized her as the older woman whose car she'd been searching. The partying wiener dogs gave her away.

"Hey, Jill, do you remember any of the doctors diagnosing a blind baby—" The administrator looked at Hunter. "Recently?"

"Couple of weeks ago?"

The woman's scowl lowered another notch. "There's no date on the paperwork?"

"Nope."

"But you've had them for *weeks*?"

Hunter did her best to look shamed. "I know, it's terrible. I had it in my car and kept forgetting to bring it up."

The older nurse was already slowly shaking her head. "I don't remember anything like that."

Hunter sighed. "Alright. I'll go get the papers. Maybe you'll be able to figure it out from those."

The woman behind the computer offered her a crisp nod. "I'm sure we will be."

Hunter turned to leave, but not before she put a hand on the wiener-dog nurse's arm. "Hey, you like mysteries, don't you? Maybe ones with a sense of humor? You should try Amy Vansant. Really good stuff."

The nurse's eyes opened wider, and she smiled. "Oh, yes, okay, thanks."

Hunter left the hospital and retrieved her shorts from the planter wall. She hopped over the low, useless fence guarding the northern end of the gated parking area and returned to her car waiting in a bank parking lot.

She retrieved her notebook and a pen to scratch out the hospital's name.

"One down, four to go."

Hers wasn't the most thorough plan, but running through the pediatric units at this rate could drop them a notch on her list of possibilities. Maybe she'd get lucky and find a nurse who remembered the blind child.

She checked her phone and saw she had a missed call.

Who could be calling me?

Voicemail.

Spammers, probably.

She played the message expecting to hear a robocall running through its paces.

"Hey, Hunter, this is Charlotte. Just a heads up, I'm following a suspicious minivan that rolled past the Bennetts' house. I'll let you know when I know more."

The girl had stationed herself outside the house as directed.

Good.

Hunter checked the tracing app on her phone. It looked as if Charlotte was parked not far from the hospital. She hadn't returned to the Bennetts' house fifteen minutes after leaving her the message, so she must have seen something interesting.

Maybe I'll swing by.

CHAPTER THIRTY-FOUR

When the sun finally rose, Charlotte checked her face in the rearview mirror of her Volvo.

I look like a crazy person.

Between getting up too early and not sleeping well the night before, she looked as if someone had dotted both her eyes.

It didn't help that surveillance was her least favorite part of being a detective and *not* the recipe for staying awake when already tired.

She closed her eyes and lowered her chin to her chest.

I'll rest my eyes for a second...

She vowed to open her eyes on every count of ten.

...nine, ten.

She looked up. *Nothing.* Just like the last four hours.

...nine, ten.

Eyes harder to open that time. She looked up.

Nothing—oh, hold on...

A minivan turned on to the Bennetts' street, and Charlotte steeled herself to be bored to tears again. The false excitement that bubbled every time a random vehicle appeared had worn her down.

She slumped down in her seat.

The minivan rolled down the street at a crawl, piquing Charlotte's interest.

Why would anyone move that slowly?

Maybe the driver lived on the street and was about to pull into a driveway...

Nope. Still coming.

The vehicle rolled past the Bennetts' house, slowing until it nearly stopped. After a weighty pause, it lurched forward and picked up speed as it departed.

The driver turned her head toward Charlotte as she passed.

Whoops.

Charlotte sat up a notch and squinted, realizing the rising sun beamed down her face like a spotlight no matter how far she tried to fold herself into the seat.

The opposite side of the street had no parking, so the situation had left her little choice. Figures—the first suspicious vehicle to go by arrived at seven a.m. when the sun sought her out like a laser pointer.

In the rearview, Charlotte watched the minivan roll through a stop sign at the end of the street and make a hurried left.

Headed for the bridge? Staying on the island?

She fired up the Volvo and made a U-turn to follow, careful to stay back in case the driver was on high alert for her vehicle after possibly spotting her inside.

Looking left at the stop sign, she watched the back of the minivan as it crossed to the opposite side of the main artery parallel to the Bennetts' street, and drove toward the bridge.

Charlotte followed, slowing twice as fast as her quarry as it approached the traffic light to allow cars to file in between them. The minivan pulled into the turn lane leading toward the bridge and off the island, but missed the signal. It rolled to a halt instead of blasting through the red light, so Charlotte decided whoever was driving wasn't in a *full-blown* panic anymore. How the woman had lurched and rolled through the stop sign caused Charlotte to expect a high-speed chase.

Charlotte slowed to allow more early-morning traffic to insert itself between her and the minivan in the turn lane, hoping the driver wouldn't spot her lurking behind. She grabbed her phone and dialed Hunter. The phone went directly to voicemail, so she left a quick message.

The light changed, and Charlotte hugged the car's bumper in front of her to be sure she made it through the light in time. Ahead of her, the minivan continued at a fast but not break-neck pace.

The more Charlotte followed, and the less the minivan tried to lose her, the more she suspected the woman had no relation to the case. The twitchy driver could be someone who read about the case in the paper and wanted a peek. From the information in the press, it wouldn't be hard for someone to find the Bennetts' address.

Maybe she was a lousy driver. There were a few of those in Florida.

Ah well. Worth a shot.

She was determined to follow the woman home and see if she had a baby in the car. Assuming she hadn't driven from Ohio to see the Bennetts' house, it wouldn't take long.

At least following someone is more exciting than staring at a house.

CHAPTER THIRTY-FIVE

Why was that woman in that car?

Kim chewed at her lip, Brody behind her, blessedly silent for a change.

There'd been a woman in that old white Volvo station wagon. She was sure of it.

Cop?

In a Volvo? Probably not. Didn't they have to use American cars by law or something?

She took a deep breath and tapped on the wheel while she waited for the light to change. She glanced in her rearview, craning her neck to search for the Volvo. She'd looked behind her at both stop signs and hadn't seen the white car following. Maybe that woman had been waiting for sunrise. There were always weird people parked near the beach.

Kim forgot about the Volvo and shifted her thoughts back to Josh Jr. Was he in that house? Did they leave him with the couple, or was he not even there?

I have to know.

How can I find out?

They weren't going to say in the paper. She'd have to break in there and look around. Her stomach lurched at the thought, but it had to be done.

Was there a camera on that gate? Could I cut through the shrubs somewhere?

She made a mental note to wear long sleeves and maybe yoga pants to keep from getting scratched.

I'll have to take a day off from work. Or not. I should do it at night, but—

Kim looked up just in time to slam on her breaks. The cars in front of her had slowed for a light.

She panted as if she'd run a race. She could hear her heart banging against her chest.

Jolted from his sleep by the sudden stop, Brody whined and bubbled like a coffee maker. She recognized it as his way of gearing up for the *real* shrieking.

Tears flowed from Kim's eyes as if a dam had given way, and she allowed herself to sob until she could barely breathe.

I can't do this anymore. I can't.

When the light changed, she hit the gas and barreled for home. Five minutes later, she pulled into her driveway, her own weeping overshadowed by Brody's bawling. It was as if he'd taken the volume of her pain as a personal challenge.

"Shut up! Shut up!"

Kim shut off the car and rested her head on the steering wheel. She needed to take a moment. She worried what she might do if she moved to get Brody out of the back now. She needed silence. A *day* of silence. She couldn't give the baby to her mother or Josh's mother for fear they'd realize it wasn't Josh Jr., but with one day of quiet, maybe she could figure out a way—

Kim looked up and gasped.

Josh stood in the driveway, hands hanging too far from his hips, as if preparing to crouch and leap on her minivan like a panther.

He looked *angry*.

Kim wiped away her tears and looked in the rearview. Her eyes glowed puffy and red. No hiding that she'd been crying.

She opened the door and slid out of the van, wondering if her legs would support her when she landed.

"What are you doing up?" she asked, turning her face away from Josh to open the back, sliding side door. Her stuffed nose made her voice sound funny, and she couldn't stop sniffing.

"Where were you?" asked Josh, his boots crunching on the gravel as he approached.

Kim reached for the crying baby, her hands shaking as she tried to unstrap him from the car seat.

"He wouldn't sleep. I thought I'd try driving him around." Kim glanced at Josh and forced a smile. "I didn't want him to wake you up."

"You've been gone an hour." Before she could gather the child in her arms, Josh grabbed her wrist and pulled her to face him. "What's wrong with your face?"

She jerked her hand from his and grabbed the baby seat to anchor herself. "Huh?"

"You're all red. You look like crap."

Go on the offensive. Sometimes that works.

"Oh sorry, Josh. I'm a little *tired*." She pulled Brody from the seat and held him against her, bobbing him up and down, hoping he'd stop crying. She couldn't hear herself think, and Josh was leaning into her, his cheeks flushed red. She imagined she could *see* the steam coming out of his ears.

"You were crying." He said, maneuvering her chin to better peer into her face.

Despite the rough way he'd gripped her chin, she could tell he was now on the fence somewhere between anger and concern. She hurried past him, cradling Brody against her chest, though his wails threatened to burst her eardrums.

"No—" Josh grabbed her arm, jerking her so hard she spun and scrambled to keep from dropping the child.

I read him wrong. He wasn't worried about me. What was that look of confusion then? What has he gotten into his head?

"Josh—"

"Don't walk away from me. What is going on?"

Kim scanned the area, worried the neighbors would call

the cops over their arguing. They'd done it before.

"Nothing, I—"

Josh's fists clenched. "You've been acting weird for weeks. Something is going on. Are you cheating on me?"

"What?"

Kim wasn't sure where the laughter came from but couldn't stop. Mouth wide, she doubled over, her whole body shaking. Josh's eyes flashed with ire, and still, she couldn't stop. She could feel wind and lights whipping by her. Her brain felt like a runaway train.

He thinks I'm cheating on him?

The truth was so much worse that it was *funny.*

Through her swollen, squinted eyes, she glanced at Josh where he stood, seemingly dumfounded, gaping back at her. Still, she couldn't stop laughing.

Something in my head broke.

Josh took a step forward. "Are you *laughing* at me?"

That's when she spotted a flash of white behind Josh and beyond the scrub pines.

Is that a car?

Did that Volvo follow me here?

Panic hit her like a wall and stopped her maniacal giggling the way Josh used his licked fingertips to snuff the candles. Her laughter pinched off, just like those darkened, glowing embers.

She spun away from her husband and ran for the back door of their home. She heard him pursue, yelling something, but she kept moving, baby Brody pressed against her chest.

CHAPTER THIRTY-SIX

The door gave way, and Kim stumbled into the house, catching herself with one hand on the stairs leading to the landing, the other hand gripping the baby tightly. She kept him pinned against her chest with his feet dangling.

When she felt a twinge in her wrist, she cried out, her arm giving way and her knee hitting the edge of the linoleum-covered step. She caught a flash of the child's legs banging against the edge of a higher step, and he screamed louder. The crack of her knee gave her enough support to scramble to her feet and make it into the kitchen. Arm bouncing off the refrigerator handle, she spun and saw Josh behind her.

Her gaze moved to the kitchen table when his hand headed in that direction. His pistol was sitting there. He'd been cleaning his gun.

A strange wet noise burbled from her lips. Not laughter this time.

What are the chances?

Nothing felt real anymore.

This can't be my life.

Two months ago, she'd been nursing Josh Jr. at that table when Josh came in and rubbed her shoulders.

I was so happy then.

Josh grabbed the gun and pointed it at her feet.

She realized he didn't want to point the weapon at his son.

*Where would the gunpoint be if he knew what she'd done—
that she was holding Brody Bennett?*

"Come here."

A jolt shot through her body.

No. Don't stop running.

She needed to get away. The house wouldn't provide her
with any shelter. At least if she was outside, there'd be a chance
a neighbor might call 911. Now wasn't the time to be
embarrassed.

Kim bolted from the kitchen, through their crumbling
lanai, and burst into the backyard through the wobbling screen
door.

Panting, she stopped in the center of their small fenced
yard and whirled as Josh appeared at the back door.

"Are you cheating on me?" he roared, striding down the
steps they'd built together out of stray bricks during happier
times. The gun hung in his hand.

"No!" she shrieked. "You're so *stupid*."

Josh jerked back his head as if she'd slapped him. "What did
you say to me?"

"You know I wouldn't cheat on you."

His chin worked without a sound for a moment, as if he
were too angry to speak. Finally, he spat out the words. "Where
were you then?"

"I—" She squeezed the baby, and he cried so hard she
worried he couldn't breathe.

"Answer me!"

Kim held the baby out in front of her, chubby legs dangling
like fish bait.

"It's him."

Josh scowled. "What the hell, Kim? *What's* him?"

"It's not him."

"What? You're not making any sense. Have you been
drinking?"

She laughed again, but not the uncontrollable giggles from earlier. She barked one sharp snort of bitter amusement and lowered herself to her knees, exhausted, the child still held out in front of her. All her energy left her. She *couldn't* remain standing.

She wanted to sleep.

"Kim, you're scaring me," said Josh.

Head hanging, she smiled. "That's funny."

"It isn't funny. What's going on?"

The truth flowed out of her as fast as her strength did.

"It isn't Josh Jr. I swapped him."

"You *what*?"

"I swapped him with this baby." Arms aching, she lowered Brody to the ground and sat him on his diaper-padded butt. "Josh was blind."

"What? What do you mean he *was* blind?"

"He *is* blind. I didn't think you'd want a blind baby. You and your sports... I thought—"

Kim looked up as Josh raised the gun again. The look on his face was one she'd never seen before. He looked like a trapped animal, his eyes wide and wild. The gun shook in his hand.

A strange calm came over Kim.

It's done. I told him. This isn't all mine now.

She felt lighter. She almost felt happy.

Now we'll go get Josh Jr. back. It's over.

"That baby in the news? You're that baby in the news?" Her husband's voice shook.

Kim pointed at baby Brody. "Are you talking to *him*?"

"Shut *up*." Josh bounced the tip of the gun up and down. "Shut up!"

She saw the muscle in his jaw clenching.

A moment before, she hadn't cared if he shot her. She'd almost *wanted* it. But now—now they could go get Josh Jr.—

"Let's go get him back. I know where he is," she said.

"Get him back? *You gave away our baby?*"

Brody lolled back against her thighs and took a breath to launch into another wail. Josh didn't look at the kid. His focus remained locked on her, the gun in his hand growing steadier.

Kim's jaw slowly creaked open.

He's going to shoot me.

CHAPTER THIRTY-SEVEN

Charlotte moved through the patch of pines beside the house. The plan hadn't been to get out of her car, but then a man she assumed to be the woman's husband came out of the house looking agitated.

Maybe agitated wasn't the right word.

He'd looked *mad*.

The two argued, and then the woman ran into the house, the man striding after her.

It looked like the woman was holding a baby. Someone had been crying, sounding more like a child than the adults.

The whole thing made Charlotte uncomfortable. She didn't want to interfere in the lives of others, but she also didn't want to sit on the curb like a lump if someone needed help. If not the woman, maybe the child. What if that *was* the Bennetts' baby? What if the woman *was* the kidnapper? Did the husband know? Is that what they were arguing about?

The woman almost looked like she'd been running a baby *away* from the man. She'd held something against her chest.

A terrible thought crossed Charlotte's mind.

Maybe he regretted the kidnapping and wanted to get rid of the evidence.

That last thought propelled Charlotte out of her Volvo. Her over-active imagination had taken the scene to its most extreme outcome, but that didn't mean it couldn't happen. She swallowed and shut the door quietly behind her.

I have to do something.

As she crept from tree to tree, the argument began anew inside the house. The words were too muffled to make out, but it was clear two adults were yelling over the almost constant wail of a baby.

Time to pick up the pace.

As Charlotte scurried to the rickety fence surrounding the property, she heard a bang, and the screaming grew louder. The baby's cries sounded as if they were just behind the fence. The man's roars were less muffled. The bang she'd heard had a familiar *smack* to it...

Screen door.

That was it. The familiar *bang!* of a sprung screen door closing behind someone. Not a threatening sound, and it meant the argument had spilled outside again.

Good. Their outdoor location would make it easier to keep an eye on things.

Charlotte spotted a gap between the rotting fence boards surrounding the property's back yard and pressed her face against it to peer through with one eye.

The woman she'd been tailing stood in the middle of an overgrown patch of grass, holding a baby to her body. Even at a distance, Charlotte could see her cheeks glistening with tears. The woman's mouth reminded her of the cartoons she'd seen as a child, where the animated characters' lips were made from rubber bands, arcing and twisting in ways a normal mouth couldn't bend.

Except when someone was crying.

The man stepped onto the porch.

"Answer me!" he barked.

Something's in his hand.

Charlotte pressed her face harder against the fence, trying to get a better view, and felt the wood pattern pressing into her flesh. The man's hand swung, obscured, behind a plant on the edge of a wooden deck.

Did I see something in his hand?

She hustled along the fence line, searching for a peephole offering a better angle. Finding one she thought could work, she pressed her eye against it.

Now she could see the man from the front. Her gaze dropped to his hand.

Gun.

The man had a gun.

Charlotte felt her stomach twist into knots and glanced back at her car.

Where her gun sat.

As usual.

Why don't I ever have it when I need it?

She knew why.

She didn't like walking around with a gun. Sure, it was a necessary tool of her trade, but she felt weird marching around with a deadly weapon strapped to her body. It seemed so *pessimistic.*

But *today* might have been a good day to be a little pessimistic.

She did have her phone.

She dialed 911.

"911, what's your emergency?" said the dispatcher.

Charlotte lowered her voice and covered her mouth with a cupped hand as she spoke into the phone. "There's a man with a gun here."

The woman on the other side of the line inquired about her safety.

"I'm safe. Can't talk," she said, trying to keep talking to a minimum.

Charlotte racked her brain for the address of the house. She'd seen it from the curb... *what was it...*

"745 Cornflower Court. Hurry."

She left the phone on and placed it on the ground.

Now what?

She wanted to distract the man from potentially killing someone, including her, but she couldn't just pop up from her side of the fence like a puppet. If she startled him, he might swing that gun at her and fire before she could talk him down.

On the other hand, she couldn't remain crouching on her side of the fence until he shot someone, either.

The woman spoke, interrupting her planning.

"It isn't Josh Jr. I swapped him."

What?

The words stopped Charlotte as easily as a bullet from that gun would have.

She is the kidnapper. That's the Bennetts' baby.

And the husband didn't know.

Charlotte felt her adrenaline building.

This could be bad. She couldn't blame the man for being mad. His wife had swapped away his baby. But she still couldn't let him shoot her. Charlotte looked at her watch. It had only been a minute since she talked to 911. It felt like a year ago.

Why did that woman have to confess now?

Certainly, she'd been safer before admitting to stealing a baby if for no other reason than her husband was less likely to fire at someone holding his child.

His, being the operative word.

Charlotte liked to think *no one* would fire in the direction of a baby, no matter what its parentage, but experience and news told her anything was possible.

She moved to the fence's gate and put her hand on the handle.

Here goes nothing.

She was about to call into the yard when she thought about the effect of a stranger's voice on a man whose whole world had just spun out of control.

She ducked down very low, so low no one would ever think to shoot there.

Hopefully. Probably.

Fingers still on the gate handle, she called out.

"Hey, neighbor!"

That sounded friendly. He would be less inclined to shoot his neighbor than a total stranger, right?

There was an awkward pause—though no gunshot—which buoyed Charlotte's hopes for a non-violent ending.

"Who's there?" the man demanded to know.

Charlotte pressed on the latch and eased the door open.

"Hi," she said, standing and poking her head around the corner. Her muscles tensed, ready to leap behind the fence if he raised his gun.

He tucked his hand behind him to hide the weapon.

Good.

"Who are you? What are you doing here?"

The husband's eyes looked dead and rimmed with red, as if he had started to cry, too.

Charlotte held up a palm. "My name's Charlotte Morgan—"

The man pulled the gun from behind his back and pointed it at her.

Nope! Not good!

Charlotte threw her back against the fence and scrambled away on all fours.

"Get back here, or I'm going to kill them both!" he screamed. He sounded like a man unhinged.

Charlotte swallowed.

I was afraid he might say something like that.

She looked at her watch again.

Two minutes since her 911 call.

Are you kidding me? Is time going backward?

"Okay. Easy. I'm coming."

Charlotte spoke slowly and crept back towards the gate. The longer it took for her to follow his directions, the better chance the police would show up before he had time to hurt anyone.

"Hurry," he said.

She raised her hands so he could see them over the fence and know she was on her way. Peering around the corner, she forced a smile.

"I'm here. We're all good," she said. She'd say there was no reason for him to be angry but decided he'd have a counterargument for that.

Now, the gun shook in his hand, which didn't help Charlotte feel better about her chances of avoiding catching lead. He looked less angry and more frightened now. She liked him better angry.

"This is none of your business," he spat. Literally. Spittle flew everywhere.

Charlotte glanced at the woman. She and the baby had stopped crying. She was shaking, too. Charlotte had the passing thought that the woman's shaking body had rocked the baby back to sleep. Being scared almost to death seemed like a rough way to get a child to sleep, but she knew mothers willing to give it a shot in a pinch.

What am I thinking? Stop.

Charlotte returned her focus to the guy with the gun.

Yeah, there you go. He's sort of important.

"It kind of *is* my business," she said. Charlotte raised her hands and stepped a little farther through the gate so he could see she wasn't armed. "I'm here for the baby."

A motion caught Charlotte's eye, and she turned to see the woman twist away from her, hiding the child from her line of sight with her body.

Does she not understand she can't keep that boy?

The man lowered the gun a little.

"Can you get Josh Jr. back?" he asked.

"Yes. Absolutely," said Charlotte, offering her most reassuring smile, though she was unsure she spoke the truth. She imagined the police and child services *would* give Josh Jr. back to the father once they confirmed he wasn't involved in the kidnapping. It might take a while.

Holding people at gunpoint didn't help his case.

"I'll tell the police you didn't have anything to do with this," she added, working her thought to its conclusion.

The gun raised again, the barrel pointing squarely at her chest.

"What about my wife?" he asked.

Charlotte's smile took a nosedive.

You mean the woman who gave away your child?

It seemed his loyalty to his wife knew no bounds. Maybe bringing up the authorities hadn't been the best idea.

"Um…" She looked at the woman, who stared back at her with wide eyes, waiting the verdict. Charlotte tried to peek at her watch, but it was too far above her.

Where are the police?

She needed to slow things down. Keep him talking. Stop saying anything that might ignite the situation.

What I need to do is take a course in hostage negotiation.

"Well, Josh—Your name is Josh, right?"

His right eye twitched. "That's none of your business."

"You told her the baby's name was Josh, Jr." piped the wife.

The man's expression exploded on his face, each feature expanding toward a different corner of his face. He swung the gun at his wife.

"You don't get to talk!" he roared.

The woman yipped and shielded the baby and her head with her arms. Appearing flustered, he trained the weapon back on Charlotte.

"What about her?" he asked again.

Charlotte's arms quivered. She lowered them a notch. "Temporary insanity? I'm sure she didn't mean to do it."

Josh rolled his eyes. "Didn't mean to do it? How do you *accidentally* steal a baby?"

He pressed his lips together in a tight, white line, his eyes growing squinty as if he were trying not to cry.

Charlotte backtracked. "I mean, no, of course it wasn't an *accident*. I just meant, she didn't *plan* it, right?"

The woman shook her head. "No, I—"

Josh's gaze shot in his wife's direction, and she slapped her hand over her mouth.

He returned his attention to Charlotte. "Who else knows?"

Crap.

Charlotte hoped he wouldn't conclude that killing *her* would end the lineup of witnesses to their kidnapping. After all, he and his wife could have gotten away with everything if she hadn't popped her head over the fence.

Time for a little hard truth.

"The police are on their way."

"What?"

"I called them. I'm an off-duty officer."

And a little lying.

Josh sneered. "No, you didn't. You're bluffing."

"I did. Josh, you don't want to shoot an officer—"

"Step in here," he said, beckoning her with the gun. He paled four shades.

Charlotte frowned, her mind racing to find another way to delay things.

If he could just hear the approaching sirens—

Josh motioned from her to the deck in front of him with his gun. "I said get in *here!*"

"She's not going in there."

The voice came from behind Charlotte. She turned as the weight of the opened gate resting against her arm lifted.

Hunter stood behind her with her weapon raised and the gun pointed at Josh.

"Put down the gun," she said aloud, and then quieter, she said to Charlotte, "Get behind me."

Charlotte felt bad putting Hunter in harm's way, but she *was* the one with the weapon. She moved aside and let Hunter step forward.

Josh swallowed and glanced at his wife.

"She didn't mean it. She'd never—"

Hunter answered him, her voice and hands steady. "I'm sure that's true, but I need you to put down the weapon."

"Are you a cop?"

"Yes."

"You are?" asked Charlotte, though, to her credit, she'd managed to say it quietly.

Hunter didn't answer, her laser focus never leaving Josh.

"Put down the weapon, take a few steps back, and sit in that chair."

Josh glanced back at a plastic patio chair behind him. He looked at his wife, and his shoulders slumped. He lowered the gun to the porch and took a few steps backward to drop into the seat, collapsing like a boneless sack of flesh.

Head lolling, his body shook with sobs.

"I'm so sorry," said his wife, her voice almost a whisper. Tears streamed down her face.

Josh showed no sign of hearing.

"Get the gun," said Hunter.

Charlotte blinked at her.

Oh right. You mean me.

She hustled around Hunter to retrieve the gun from the porch.

"You, come here," said Hunter to the woman. She'd lowered her gun and motioned with her opposite hand.

"Can I go to him?" asked the woman, looking at Josh.

"Not right now. Bring me the baby."

After a hesitation, the woman walked forward with the child. She handed him to Hunter.

"What's your name?" asked Hunter.

"Kim."

"Okay, Kim. I need you to stay here against this fence."

Charlotte returned with the gun. In the distance, sirens wailed.

"Take him," said Hunter, handing her the baby.

"What?"

Without thinking, Charlotte put out an arm, and Hunter tucked the baby into the crook of it. In her other hand, she still held Josh's gun. Josh sat sobbing on the porch, shoulders heaving with growing intensity. Kim had slid to a squat, her back against the fence, saying "I'm sorry" over and over, her hands covering her face.

"Police are here. Don't let them near each other," said Hunter pointing from Josh to Kim before walking the fence line away from her.

"Wait, where are you—?"

Without stopping, Hunter turned, put her fingers to her lips, smiled, and then disappeared around the fence.

Charlotte stood staring at the space Hunter had occupied, baby in one hand, gun in the other, the air filled with police sirens and sobbing.

She looked down at Brody.

"What just happened?"

The baby gurgled and tried to shove his own blue-socked toes into his mouth.

CHAPTER THIRTY-EIGHT

"And then she just walked away?" asked Angelina.

Charlotte nodded.

"Why didn't you tackle her?" asked Croix from behind the desk. She reminded Charlotte of the old guys from *The Muppet Show*, constantly heckling her from their booth.

She shifted her eyes in Croix's direction.

"How was I supposed to tackle her with a baby in one hand and a gun in the other?"

Croix shrugged and muttered as she turned away to busy herself with paperwork. "I could have done it."

"Siofra would have kicked her butt anyway," said Angelina.

Charlotte sucked her eye tooth with her tongue. "Thank you. Thank you for your confidence and support."

Though she was sure Angelina was right.

"Anyway, I still don't know if she *was* Siofra."

Angelina held Harley in front of her face and booped the dog's impossibly tiny nose against her own. "We do. We *know* it was Aunt Siofra, don't we, Harley-girl?" she sang in a baby voice. Harley's tiny butt trembled with happiness, spurred on by her wagging tail. When Angelina set her on the desk, her tiny nails tap-danced with joy.

Charlotte sighed. It had been a long night. The police had naturally wanted to talk to her for hours. She told the truth without sharing *every* detail. She didn't mention the mystery woman who swept in like Superman to save the day might be her aunt. She shared that she thought the woman worked for the Bennetts. She imagined if Hunter wanted credit for her intervention, she'd get it from them, and if the cops wanted to find her, they could start there.

She still couldn't figure out how Hunter had known where she was.

She must have been following me.

Did Hunter not trust her to work her half of the plan while she checked the hospitals?

Making idle chit-chat with one of the police officers between interviews, she heard Baby Brody had reunited with his parents, and Josh Jr. had been sent to the father's parents until everything could be sorted. She didn't know *what* would happen to the mother. It seemed clear to Charlotte the woman had suffered some sort of breakdown, but she was sure the authorities wouldn't let her walk after she stole a baby.

Charlotte was eager to get back to the Inn, where, exhausted, she slept until nine when the sound of Angelina's heels clicking outside her door woke her up. She suspected the noise had been on purpose. She wanted to hear what happened with Hunter.

She took a quick shower and dressed, thinking about how much she wanted to share with Angelina and how much she really *knew*.

Did she want to stay and look for her aunt?

No.

Her time at the Loggerhead Inn had come to an end.

The elevator doors parted, and she entered the lobby, checking the time on the sea-turtle-shaped clock hanging behind Croix's head. *Eleven a.m.* She could be back in Pineapple Port by two if she left now.

"It's about time, sleepyhead," muttered Angelina from her desk.

Charlotte chuckled and opened the location app on her

phone to see if Declan was at work. Spotting a new name in her list of connections, she gasped.

"What is it?" asked Angelina.

"Hunter's been tracking my phone."

"What?"

"She turned on the locating app and approved her connection on my phone."

Angelina's brow knit. "How did she do that? She stole your phone?"

"No. I gave it to her." Charlotte thought back to handing Hunter her phone at the dock.

She must have done it then.

Smooth.

"We'd just met. It never even occurred to me she'd already be plotting ways to track me—"

Croix scoffed. When Charlotte turned to look at her, she looked away, shuffling papers.

"So you're checking out? You're not going to stay and try and find her?" Angelina's gaze dropped to settle on the duffle bag laying at Charlotte's feet.

Charlotte shook her head.

"No. If she wants to be found, she'll show up." She glanced back at Croix. "Plus, you have people here *much* savvier than me if you want to find her."

The sound of the sarcasm dripping from her words made Croix look up.

"Agreed," she drawled.

Charlotte held up her phone. "Plus, she can find me anytime she likes."

Angelina grinned. "You're not going to turn off the tracking?"

"Nah. Maybe she'll come to me."

"It doesn't work both ways? You can't track her?"

"No. She'd have to approve my request to track her. But that's a good idea." Charlotte submitted a request and stared at her phone to see if anything happened.

Nothing.

She clicked on Declan's phone and discovered he wasn't at work. He was at *her* house.

"That's weird," she mumbled.

"What?" asked Angelina.

"Oh, nothing. My boyfriend is at my house. I thought he'd be at work by now."

Angelina shrugged. "He probably misses you."

Charlotte laughed. "Right. He's sitting in my living room pining for me, smelling my clothes."

Angelina tucked Harley under her arm and stood from her place behind the concierge desk. She thrust out her other hand and motioned for Charlotte to come in for a hug.

"Well, it's been nice meeting you. If Siofra visits, you'll be the first to know."

Charlotte gave her a sideways hug and picked up her duffle bag. By the time she'd straightened, Croix had appeared in front of her, her hand thrust out to shake.

"See ya," she said.

Charlotte shook her hand. "See ya."

She moved toward the exit. Bracco spotted her coming and opened the door for her.

"It was nice to meet you, Bracco," she said as she lugged her duffle through the door.

He touched the brim of his cap.

"Yep."

She stopped and smiled.

He said the right word.

Unwilling to ruin the moment, she nodded and kept moving without pressing for more.

The drive to Pineapple Port proved more brutal than the trip to the east coast had been. Charlotte found herself stuck behind two local trucks going *exactly* the speed limit through the pasture lands of middle Florida and, later, one tractor going twenty miles *less* than the speed limit. Luckily, the green behemoth didn't stay on the road long, but it slowed her time. It took her three hours and thirteen minutes instead of the two-fifty-five she'd managed in the other direction.

Excited to surprise Declan, she didn't call to warn him she was on her way. She checked her phone as she neared Charity and found him *still* at her house.

Odd. She guessed he'd gone to get something for Abby and accidentally left his phone there. He was probably going crazy looking for it.

She pulled to her house to find Declan's car parked at the curb.

An enormous man was on her roof.

She squinted through her sunglasses.

Why is there a giant on my roof?

It had to be Blade, Declan's employee. No one else was that big.

She suspected Declan had asked Blade to help him fix her leaky roof. She took a few steps back to get a better view and saw half the shingles missing.

Wandering towards her door, her eyes still locked on Blade, she narrowly avoided tripping over a pile of roofing tiles.

"Hey, Blade," she said.

"Hey, Miss Charlotte," said the giant of a man, grinning down at her.

"Did Declan hire you to fix my roof?"

She heard his great baritone laugh. "Eventually."

Eventually?

"What does that mean?"

"I'll let him tell you."

"Is he inside?"

Blade looked down at the roof around him and then nodded. "Yep."

Charlotte went inside to be greeted by her bouncing Wheaton.

"I told you I'd be back. I always come back," she said, squatting to receive her sloppy kisses.

Declan appeared at the end of her hall, looking sweaty and flustered, his eyes wide.

"What are you doing here?"

She laughed and straightened. "I live here."

"Yeah, but—"

"What's going on?"

"Uh..." His gaze bounced in the direction from which he'd come.

"You're fixing my roof?" she prompted, moving in to kiss him hello. "I mean, you hired Blade?"

She lifted her arms to hug him and then thought better of it. His face shone with sweat, and his shirt looked like he'd just stepped out of the ocean. Tiny white flecks covered his arms.

"Why are you so sweaty?" As she said the words, she realized the house *felt* a lot warmer than usual. She plucked at his shirt. "What's all this white stuff stuck to you?'

He grimaced. "Um, funny story..."

She scowled.

Something is definitely wrong.

She glanced down the hall toward her bedroom, and he held up his palms.

"Before you go in there, I should warn you—"

Charlotte moved past him and strode to her bedroom. Her bed looked more like a hot tub than a bed. Water pooled in the center and dripped to the floor around it. Bedding clumped in the corner like a soggy beanbag chair. Saw horses stood perpendicular to the wall, where someone had been cutting drywall.

A gigantic square in the ceiling hovered over her bed. She

moved toward it and peered up.

She saw daylight.

Like an approaching eclipse, the daylight disappeared, replaced by Blade's smiling face. He waved.

"Hi, Miss Charlotte."

She turned to Declan, her jaw slack.

"What happened?"

The corner of his mouth curled up in a sheepish smile. "The best of intentions went awry."

"*You* tried to fix my leak?"

He nodded. "I looked for it where you said it was."

She pointed to the hole in her ceiling. "But it wasn't *here*. I traced it along the beam in the attic. I think the real leak is closer to the peak."

He ran his hand through his sweaty hair, leaving a spotty trail of gypsum flecks. "Yeah. Mariska let me know that. A little late."

She looked at her bed and the bedding in the corner. "But that doesn't explain why everything is soaked?"

"It rained while I was up there. *Hard*."

Charlotte paused as she recounted their previous phone conversation. "Is that why you asked me if old men check the weather every morning?"

He nodded. "Bob and the others knew a storm was coming, but they thought it would be funnier to watch me work than to warn me."

Charlotte burst out laughing. "He stood there and watched you work?"

"Sat. They had chairs."

"*They*?"

"Bob, Frank, George..." Declan sighed and put his hands on his hips. He looked annoyed and amused at the same time. "They got me good."

"Oh, you poor thing." She decided to brave the sweat and give him a hovering hug. He squeezed her back and then let her escape from his damp body.

"There's more," he said.

"More?"

He nodded. "In my haste to get off the roof and away from the lightning, I stepped too close to the hole and broke through."

"Making the hole *bigger* for the rain."

"Exactly. I tried to cover the hole with trash bags, but the wind made it almost impossible."

"Not to mention the lightning," she added.

"That too. By the time I'd bought a tarp and got back, the rain was over, and—" He spread his hands, sweeping across her watery room. "Ta da."

Charlotte noticed a wad of trash bags stuffed inside a large bucket, and he followed her gaze there with his own.

"Turns out water collects on plastic bags covering a hole until the weight pulls it into the house with one big *sploosh*."

She studied the dark circles under his eyes. "You look as tired as me."

His shoulders slumped. "You have no idea."

She patted him on the arm. "I'm just glad you're okay. I will talk with Bob about leaving you on a roof in the lightning."

Declan chuckled. "To his credit, he *did* check to make sure my metal hammer had a wooden handle."

"Oh. Well, in that case, never mind. He's a prince among men."

Declan grinned and took a deep breath.

"Anyway, Blade and I will get everything all fixed up. You and Abby can stay at my place tonight."

Charlotte tapped him on the chest. "I think that's been your plan all along."

"*Right*. This seemed like the most efficient way to get you to sleep over."

She laughed. "No problem. And thank you for trying. That was sweet of you."

He blushed. "I should have known better than to try." He

cocked his head. "So wait, why are *you* so tired? Anything happen?"

She was about to answer when her phone buzzed. Charlotte pulled it from her pocket and glanced at the screen.

Hunter had accepted her tracking app request.

She was still in Jupiter Beach, not far from the Loggerhead Inn.

She smiled and looked up at Declan.

"I think I have an aunt."

~~ THE END ~~

WANT SOME MORE? FREE PREVIEW!

If you liked this book, read on for a preview of the next Pineapple Port Mystery AND the Shee McQueen Mystery-Thriller Series (which shares characters with the Pineapple Port world!)

THANK YOU!

Thank you for reading! If you enjoyed this book, please swing back to Amazon and leave me a review — even short reviews help authors like me find new fans!

GET A FREE STORY

Find out about Amy's latest releases and get a free story by joining her newsletter! http://www.AmyVansant.com

ABOUT THE AUTHOR

USA Today and Wall Street Journal bestselling author Amy Vansant has written over 20 books, including the fun, thrilling Shee McQueen series, the rollicking, twisty Pineapple Port Mysteries, and the action-packed Kilty urban fantasies. Throw in a couple romances and a YA fantasy for her nieces...

Amy specializes in fun, exciting reads with plenty of laughs and action -- she tried to write serious books, but they always ended up full of jokes, so she gave up.

Amy lives in Jupiter, Florida with her muse/husband a goony Bordoodle named Archer.

BOOKS BY AMY VANSANT

Pineapple Port Mysteries
Funny, clean & full of unforgettable characters

Shee McQueen Mystery-Thrillers
Action-packed, fun romantic mystery-thrillers

Kilty Urban Fantasy/Romantic Suspense
Action-packed romantic suspense/urban fantasy

Slightly Romantic Comedies
Classic romantic romps

The Magicatory
Middle-grade fantasy

FREE PREVIEW

PINEAPPLE HURRICANE

A Pineapple Port Mystery: Book Eleven – By Amy Vansant

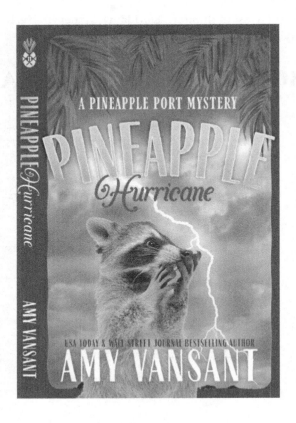

CHAPTER ONE

Sheriff Frank Marshal guided his cruiser to the curb of a gray modular home located a few blocks south of his own in the Pineapple Port fifty-five-plus community. He hated getting calls about his own neighborhood. Even a simple robbery like a missing lawn ornament put him on edge for weeks. He'd start peering through his windows at intermittent intervals each night, scanning the darkness for the juvenile delinquents responsible.

The missing lawn ornaments were almost always taken by juvenile delinquents. They liked to pose and dress them up for social media posts. His own fishing frog had been forced to wear a wig and perform lewd yoga poses in locations all over the county before the thief's mother finally turned in the little brat.

Lawn ornament molestation was bad enough. This time, instead of someone losing a stone alligator or a gazing ball, someone had *found* a person, possibly dead. *In Pineapple Port.* He held his breath, waiting to hear the address crackle over the radio. When it did, shoulders he didn't realize he'd bunched, released.

He didn't recognize the address.

No one I know.

Frank flipped off his siren. A Hispanic woman stood on the sidewalk outside the home, pointing towards the house with increasing urgency as he folded himself out of the car.

"Did you call an ambulance?" he asked, hustling as fast as his aging legs would move him.

The woman shook her head, her eyes wide with what looked like both fear and confusion. "No. Es *muerto*."

"Marto who?"

"*Muerto*."

"Okay. It doesn't matter what his name is. Where is he?"

"Alrededor del costado de la casa."

Frank perked.

Casa. I know that one.

"Ah, in the house, got it," he said, pleased with himself for frequenting Taco Casa enough to pick up a smattering of the language.

Frank entered the home through the wide open front door.

Whoever Marto is, he's going to be furious when he finds out someone let out all his air-conditioning.

"Where?" he asked the woman who'd followed him inside. She seemed frustrated, waving her hands in the air, when she said, "No aquí."

"I don't need a key, the door is wide open."

"*No*, over there," she pointed while hooking her arm out and around, as if she were trying to hug a bear. Frank realized she meant around the outside of the house.

"Outside?"

"Si."

"Got it."

He trotted back down the front steps and around the side of the house to find a man lying on the ground at the foot of a tall ladder. The dead man lay on his stomach, his head turned away from Frank's view, but otherwise straight and proper, every snow-white hair in place. If he'd been bare-chested and not stretched across his muddy, ant-ridden lawn, he could have been tanning, getting a little color on his back.

Frank only needed to touch the body to know help had

arrived too late. Even in the morning sun, the old man's flesh felt cold. He wore what looked like work shorts, cargo-style, stained with multi-colored paint blotches, as if this pair had been his go-to outfit for home projects. Walking around the opposite side of the body, Frank saw the man's lips were blue, his cheeks the color of a fish's belly.

Frank's gaze climbed up the ladder propped against the side of the house and back down to the body.

Cause of death seemed pretty obvious.

"Hello?"

Frank heard a familiar voice calling from the front of the house.

"Around the side," he shouted.

Charlotte Morgan appeared, long brown ponytail swinging, their resident neighborhood orphan-turned-detective. As usual, she seemed unable to hide the spring in her step.

The girl loves crimes. And a body... Boy, this is her lucky day.

He'd let Charlotte shadow him during her private eye training and allowed her to help investigate the scene of a suspicious death. He'd never seen anyone so happy to poke around a dead guy. That case had been a little strange, and he'd assumed *that* was why she seemed so excited, but seeing her now, fighting to look somber—he had to wonder if *any* old body made her day.

He also had to wonder if she'd bugged his cruiser. Every time he had a case more interesting than graffiti, Charlotte managed to show up moments after he did.

"Hey, I heard the sirens—oh. Hm." Charlotte's gaze dropped to the dead man. Her lips curled into a tiny smile and then dropped as if someone had turned on the gravity.

Frank chuckled to himself.

Nice try. I saw that.

He motioned to the ladder. "I hate to be the one to break it to you, but this one's an accident."

Charlotte scowled. "Very funny. It's bad enough a man died

here, Frank. I'm not hoping it's a *murder*."

"Uh huh."

Charlotte seemed to notice the Hispanic woman for the first time and flashed her an empathic smile.

"Are you his wife?"

The woman looked offended. "No. House cleaning."

"She found the body," explained Frank, before turning his attention to the housekeeper. "What's your name, ma'am?"

"Corentine Flores."

"Do you know him?"

She shook her head. "No. First time here."

"He left quite a first impression," mumbled Charlotte trying to peer around Frank to get a better look at the body. He stepped in front of her and grunted with disapproval.

Frank continued his interview. "You found him like this?"

"Muerto," she said, nodding.

Frank mumbled to Charlotte. "I think his name is Marty and she calls him *Marto*, near as I can figure."

"Muerto means *dead*," said Charlotte, ever helpful. She motioned at a square, canvas casing on the ground. "Looks like he was trying to cover his skylights for the hurricane."

Frank heaved a sigh. "Why these old people crawl up on their roofs like they're still twenty, I'll never know."

Charlotte used Frank's attention on the ladder to move around him and squat beside the body. "I guess he thought he could do it. I mean, when do you *know* you're too old to do something?"

"When you fall and kill yourself," muttered Frank.

He turned back to the woman. "When did you find him? You called right away?"

She nodded.

"Do you have any idea when he fell?"

The woman shook her head and her expression dropped, as if she felt guilty for being unable to help more than she could.

Poor thing. She's probably had quite a shock.

"It hasn't been too long. There's no lividity," said Charlotte. She wrapped her hand in her shirt and shifted the man's arm. "He's in rigor, so three, four hours?"

"Can you not touch him please?" said Frank.

"But I covered my hand, and you said yourself, it isn't a crime scene."

"It's still creepy. Just cut it out."

Another police car arrived and lanky Deputy Daniel soon strolled over to the group.

Late and useless as usual.

"Thought you might need some help," he said. He was talking to Frank but his eyes were on Charlotte. Frank stepped into his frame of view.

"*You.* Listen up. Call the coroner for me."

Daniel snapped out of his Charlotte-induced trance. "Huh? Oh. Yeah, sure..." He tipped his hat at Charlotte as she looked up and acknowledged his presence. Daniel beamed.

Charlotte held up a hand. "Hold the phone. Stop the presses."

Frank put his hands on his hips. "I can't let you play *crime scene* with this guy all day long. We need to call the coroner."

"It's not that. I think it might not be an accident."

"What? Wishful thinking doesn't make it so, sweetheart. He fell off the damn roof. He did everything but leave a note that said *I'm going to fall off the roof now.*"

"But I think he *did* leave a note."

"That he wrote on the way down?"

"Oh, I don't know," said Charlotte, looking smug. "I don't know if he had time to do that *and* eat it."

Frank closed his eyes and prayed for strength. "Will you make some sense?"

"Come here. Look."

Frank moved around to Charlotte's side of the body and squinted toward where she pointed near the man's mouth. He could see now something beige rested between his lips.

"That his dentures? Popped out of his mouth maybe?"

"Put your glasses on. It looks like cloth."

Frank felt inside his shirt pocket for his eyeglasses and slipped them on his face to peer again at the object pressed between the man's lips.

"What is it?" asked Daniel.

"Make yourself useful and get me a pair of gloves out of your car," said Frank.

Dan jogged to his trunk and returned with two pairs of latex gloves.

"I've got the gloves," he announced, as if he'd just found the cure for the common cold.

Frank shook his head and took a pair.

I guess when you're that useless fetching gloves is a win.

"Thank you," said Charlotte, reaching up for the second pair.

Daniel's chest puffed another inch.

Frank slipped on the gloves and peeled open the man's blue lips. Pinching the edge of the flat object he slid out a round, cloth disk with a stitched edge. At the top of its design, sat a yellow plus-sign, a blue house occupied the lower left corner, and the lower right sported what looked like green lightning.

"What is this?" he asked aloud.

"More importantly, how did it get in his mouth? Hold it still, let me get a picture." Charlotte pulled her ever-present phone from her pocket and snapped a photo.

Frank addressed Corentine. "Ma'am, I'm afraid we're going to have to ask you to stick around. Do you understand?"

The woman wrapped her hand around the waterspout and rested her shoulder on the wall, resigned to waiting.

Frank returned to musing on the mysterious patch. "Maybe his hands were full and he needed a way to hold this while he was on the ladder."

"But why would he need a patch on a roof?" asked Charlotte poking at her phone.

"What are you doing?"

"I'm doing an online image search. Here it is." She held the phone up for Frank to see. "It's an emergency preparedness Boy Scout badge."

"Huh," said Frank. The badge on Charlotte's phone *did* look exactly like the one in his own hand, but for the traces of watery blood on his version.

"How did they solve any crimes before the Internet?" she asked no one in particular.

"No Internet *and* we were all so busy hunting dinosaurs," said Frank, rising. He gazed up the ladder. "You think he was going to award himself a patch for putting on the hurricane covers?"

"You're suggesting he's the world's oldest boy scout?"

"I dunno. People are weird. Nothing surprises me anymore."

"I think it's more likely someone left a message."

"Oh you and the murderers."

She shrugged and Frank looked at Dan. "Skip the ambulance. Call in the FDLE."

Dan nodded and jogged back to his cruiser.

"Florida Department of Legal Eagles?" asked Charlotte.

Frank chuckled. "So, you don't know everything after all. It's Florida Department of Law Enforcement. They'll need to take a look. Sheriff's department doesn't have the resources for a full-blown investigation."

"But you have *me*."

"Right. My mistake, cancel that order." He threw out an arm and pulled Charlotte to him for a quick side-hug and she giggled.

She's so adorable.

Frank stretched his back with another, deeper groan and by the time he'd looked back down, Charlotte had the corpse's head in her gloved hands, lifting it to peek underneath it.

"Hey, put that down. I've officially declared this a

suspicious death."

"Sorry." Charlotte set the dead man's head back down and stood. "It's definitely suspicious."

"Man's got a Boy Scout patch in his mouth. Of course it's suspicious."

"And that other thing…"

Frank sighed. "Fine. You already cost me a ton of paperwork finding that patch. What *other* thing is going to complicate my life?"

Charlotte's eyes lit with excitement. "I thought you'd never ask."

Frank tried not to laugh. If he ever revealed how much her quests for the truth amused and impressed him, she might end up twice as tenacious.

Charlotte pointed at the man's head. "It looks like he has a massive cut on his skull."

"That's your big reveal? He fell off a *roof*."

"But look." Charlotte jumped up and down as if she were on a trampoline, stopping to look exasperated by his befuddled silence.

"Look at how springy the grass is," she said.

Frank found himself distracted by a different oddity.

All that jumping and she doesn't sound winded.

Frank couldn't remember the last time he did something that active without collapsing into a chair afterwards.

"So?" he asked.

"So, it's too soft for him to have the deep smashy mess he has there."

"*Smashy*? Is that an official detective word?"

"It is now. It looks like there's bits of masonry in there. Red like brick…"

She drifted off, and Frank felt certain she was accessing some sort of gravel database in her brain, trying to find a match.

"I'm sure there are bits of rock down there under the grass," he said, pointing at the ground.

"Yes, but it isn't that kind. It's more like—" She looked around before wandering toward the back of the house.

When she didn't immediately return, Frank sniffed.

Okay. Nice talk.

Hearing footsteps behind him, he turned to find Daniel returning.

"Where'd Charlotte go?" he asked.

"Who knows." Frank turned to the housekeeper, who was still standing at the corner of the house, wide-eyed and watching.

"You know a little Spanish, don't you, Dan?"

Daniel grinned as if he had a secret no one else knew. "Un poco."

"Okay. Could you un poco her statement from her?"

"Sure." Daniel pulled his notepad out of his belt as if every page said *Deputy Dan is Super Cool!* and swaggered over to the woman.

That'll keep them busy until FDLE gets here. Now I just have to get Charlotte out of here before—

"Brick!" called a voice from the back yard.

Frank took a cleansing breath and strolled around the house to find Charlotte pointing triumphantly at a brick lying in a muddy corner of the yard.

He licked his lips and stared down at the brick. "Dare I ask?"

"Blood." She leaned down to point at a brown stain marring the edge of the brick.

Frank pulled his glasses from his head and lowered himself to a squat to inspect the stain.

"Could be dirt," he said.

"Could be *blood*."

It does look like blood. Still…

"So you think he fell on the brick and then made it as far as the ladder before he collapsed?"

Frank knew the chances of his fanciful scenario being what

Charlotte suspected were about as likely as him standing back up without his knees cracking like Chinese New Year.

"*No.* I think someone hit him with the brick and tried to make it look like he fell off the roof."

He sighed. "Anyone ever tell you you're a pain in the neck?"

She smiled and Frank held up a hand.

"My knees locked up."

Charlotte helped him to stand straight, and they headed toward the front of the house.

"Why couldn't you take up mahjong like the other ladies? Why do you always have to make my life so difficult?"

"Sorry. I'm afraid you were always my hero. Not Mrs. Terry."

I'm her hero?

Frank felt his throat tighten. "Who's Mrs. Terry?" he asked, trying to change the subject before his eyes teared.

"She's the best mahjong player in Pineapple Port."

"Right." He swallowed hard. "Just my luck."

CHAPTER TWO

"Sounds like we're going to get a direct hit," said Darla as she and Mariska selected Publix shopping carts. They jostled hips, each trying to avoid the cart with the wonky leg, its wheel hovering three inches off the ground like a levitating magician.

With a grunt, Mariska jerked her cart clear of its nested mates. "Stupid hurricane. The thing is crazy. It's headed for Texas, then Louisiana, then back at Texas, and now *here*."

"Staggering like a drunk," agreed Darla. "They should have named it after my ex-husband."

"Which one?"

Darla shrugged. "Take your pick."

They pushed their way towards the first aisle. Mariska stopped to check a display for BOGO wine, tucking tight to the bottles to avoid other shoppers. She didn't drink wine, but how could she avoid a *buy one get one free*? To *not* buy a bottle would be losing money.

"It's busy for this time of day," she mumbled.

Darla agreed.

Plucking a bottle from the shelf to read its description, Mariska's elbow grazed the shirt of a man rustling through plastic boxes of strawberries. He'd stood so close to her she could feel the heat radiating off of him.

Anger bubbled in her chest.

Who are all these people? This is my store.

Agitated, she wheeled away from the display and found Darla parked in front of the shredded cheeses. She clucked her tongue, staring daggers at a woman whose cart caromed towards her own.

"Why are so many people here?"

Darla shrugged. "I don't know. I thought all the snowbirds left."

"Idiots. We should have come earlier." Darla tossed two packages of BOGO bacon into her cart. Publix offered one brand or another buy-one-get-one-free every week, so between the two of them, Darla and Mariska had close to twenty packages of bacon in their freezers. Trapped by a hurricane, they'd die of high blood pressure and salt intake *long* before they ever died of starvation.

Darla cocked her head like a curious beagle. "Hey..."

"Hm?" Mariska read the back of a package of fat-free cream cheese knowing she had every intention of buying the full-fat package.

"The eggs are all gone."

"What?" Mariska turned to see a system of shelves she'd never realized existed. They'd always been covered with cartons of eggs.

"What happened?" she asked.

"I don't know..."

Mariska watched a woman roll by with a child in her cart, the boy barely visible over multiple packages of toilet paper and paper towels.

"She's going to lose that kid in there."

"These empty shelves remind me of the last time a hurricane..." Darla's voice trailed off as another woman stormed by with at least a dozen packages of ground beef.

"Oh no," she said.

"What?" Marla followed her friend's gaze to the passing cart. "Why is she—oh *no*."

Mariska and Darla's gazes met.

"*Panic-buying*," they said in unison.

Darla set her jaw. "*Snowbirds*. First they clog up our highway, then they swarm our beaches like nasty little ants, and then they steal all our food."

Mariska shook a fist. "Usually we only have to deal with snowbirds *or* hurricanes, not *both*. This early storm is for the *birds*."

"*Snowbirds*."

They giggled.

Darla sobered. "Okay. We're going to have to do this like a military operation. I'll hit the paper products, you hit the milk."

Mariska craned her neck to see around the growing crowd. The refrigerated bins, once overflowing with chicken, beef and pork, glowed naked and white like empty rib cages.

"It's all gone," she whispered, her tone implying she'd lost a friend.

Darla's shoulders slumped. "We're too late."

"But the hurricane only turned track towards us *this morning*. It probably won't even hit us."

Darla gritted her teeth so hard Mariska worried she'd crack a tooth.

"What is *wrong* with these people?"

"It's like they lose their minds. You'd better get a move on to the paper products. I'll meet you there."

Darla saluted Mariska and took off, shamelessly sprinting her cart in the direction of aisle eight.

"Water!" Mariska called after her.

Mariska hustled to the meat, barely slowing to snatch the last bottle of her favorite coffee creamer from the shelf as if she'd been training for a Coffemate emergency all her life.

She stared with dismay at the empty meat shelves. Nothing remained except hot Italian sausage and corned beef set out for St. Patrick's day—the one day a year people choked down corned beef in order to get back to drinking.

She grabbed the sausage, thinking *lasagna,* and pushed toward the paper product aisle. There, she found Darla standing with several other women, all of them gaping at empty shelves, seemingly shellshocked.

"All gone," said Darla as Mariska approached.

The four of them stood there a moment longer recognizing a moment of silence, until one of the women spoke aloud.

"*Potatoes.*"

She slapped her hand over her mouth, realizing her mistake.

The women looked at each other, eyes wide with panicked determination. Leaping to action, three carts collided. Darla dodged them at the last second and skated by.

"I'll get you a bag!" she called behind her as she torqued the cart around the corner headed for more produce.

"Get lettuce!" screamed Mariska.

Get *Pineapple Hurricane* on Amazon!

ANOTHER FREE PREVIEW!

THE GIRL WHO WANTS

A Shee McQueen Mystery-Thriller by Amy Vansant

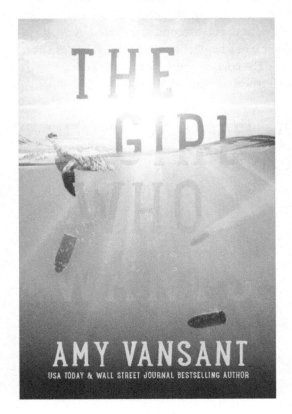

CHAPTER ONE

Three Weeks Ago, Nashua, New Hampshire.

Shee realized her mistake the moment her feet left the grass.

He's enormous.

She'd watched him drop from the side window of the house. He landed four feet from where she stood, and still, her brain refused to register the warning signs. The nose, big and lumpy as breadfruit, the forehead some beach town could use as a jetty if they buried him to his neck...

His knees bent to absorb his weight and *her* brain thought, *got you.*

Her brain couldn't be bothered with simple math: *Giant, plus Shee, equals Pain.*

Instead, she jumped to tackle him, dangling airborne as his knees straightened and the *pet the rabbit* bastard stood to his full height.

Crap.

The math added up pretty quickly after that.

Hovering like Superman mid-flight, there wasn't much she could do to change her disastrous trajectory. She'd *felt* like a superhero when she left the ground. Now, she felt more like a Canada goose staring into the propellers of Captain Sully's Airbus A320.

She might take down the plane, but it was going to *hurt.*

Frankenjerk turned toward her at the same moment she plowed into him. She clamped her arms around his waist like a little girl hugging a redwood. Lurch returned the embrace, twisting her to the ground. Her back hit the dirt and air burst from her lungs like a double shotgun blast.

Ow.

Wheezing, she punched upward, striking Beardless Hagrid in the throat.

That didn't go over well.

Grabbing her shoulder with one hand, Dickasaurus flipped her on her stomach like a sausage link, slipped his hand under her chin and pressed his forearm against her windpipe.

The only air she'd gulped before he cut her supply stank of damp armpit. He'd tucked her cranium in his arm crotch, much like the famous noggin-less horseman once held his severed head. Fireworks exploded in the dark behind her eyes.

That's when a thought occurred to her.

I haven't been home in fifteen years.

What if she died in Gigantor's armpit? Would her father even know?

Has it really been that long?

Flopping like a landed fish, she forced her assailant to adjust his hold and sucked a breath as she flipped on her back. Spittle glistened on his lips, his brow furrowed as if she'd asked him to read a paragraph of big-boy words.

His nostrils flared like the Holland Tunnel.

There's an idea.

Making a V with her fingers, Shee thrust upward, stabbing into his nose, straining to reach his tiny brain.

Goliath roared. Jerking back, he grabbed her arm to unplug her fingers from his nose socket. She whipped away her limb before he had a good grip, fearing he'd snap her bones with his Godzilla paws.

Kneeling before her, he clamped both hands over his face, cursing as blood seeped from behind his fingers.

Shee's gaze didn't linger on that mess. Her focus fell to his crotch, hovering a foot above her feet, protected by nothing but a thin pair of oversized sweatpants.

Scrambled eggs, sir?

She kicked.

He howled.

Shee scuttled back like a crab, found her feet and snatched her gun from her side. The gun she should have pulled *before* trying to tackle the Empire State Building.

"Move a muscle and I'll aerate you," she said. She always liked that line.

The golem growled, but remained on the ground like a good dog, cradling his family jewels.

Shee's partner in this manhunt, a local cop easier on the eyes than he was useful, rounded the corner and drew his own weapon.

She smiled and holstered the gun he'd lent her. Unknowingly.

"Glad you could make it."

Her portion of the operation accomplished, she headed toward the car as more officers swarmed the scene.

"Shee, where are you going?" called the cop.

She stopped and turned.

"Home, I think."

His gaze dropped to her hip.

"Is that my gun?"

Get *The Girl Who Wants* on Amazon!

Made in the USA
Coppell, TX
06 November 2023